"You've ruined half a day's filming!"

Ryan's fury grew as he stormed on. "The idea of bringing you along was mine; I argued that money could be saved by having script alterations done on the spot. I do not expect to be proved wrong. So we can't afford the expense or inconvenience of having you continuously late!"

"That's right, blame me for all your mistakes!" Hanna exclaimed furiously. "I've explained about the car breakdown. I've apologized. What more can I do?"

"Perhaps the biggest mistake was bringing you at all!"

She gasped. "How can you be such a hypocrite? I didn't want to come anyway—"

"Rubbish!"

" —mainly because I knew I couldn't possibly work with *you*!" Hanna clamped her mouth shut. It was best to let him think the problem was professional and not personal.

WELCOME
TO THE WONDERFUL WORLD
OF *Harlequin Presents*

Interesting, informative and entertaining,
each Harlequin romance portrays an appealing
and original love story. With a varied array
of settings, we may lure you on an African safari,
to a quaint Welsh village, or an exotic Riviera
location—anywhere and everywhere that adventurous
men and women fall in love.

As publishers of Harlequin romances, we're
extremely proud of our books. Since 1949,
Harlequin Enterprises has built its publishing
reputation on the solid base of quality and
originality. Our stories are the most popular
paperback romances sold in North America; every
month, eight new titles are released and sold at
nearly every book-selling store in Canada and the
United States.

A free catalogue listing all available Harlequin romances
can be yours by writing to the

HARLEQUIN READER SERVICE
1440 South Priest Drive, Tempe, AZ 85281
Canadian address: Stratford, Ontario N5A 6W2

We sincerely hope you enjoy reading
this Harlequin Presents.

Yours truly,

THE PUBLISHERS

PAMELA POPE

the magnolia siege

Harlequin Books

TORONTO · LONDON · LOS ANGELES · AMSTERDAM
SYDNEY · HAMBURG · PARIS · STOCKHOLM · ATHENS · TOKYO

For
Ruth and Neil

———————————

Harlequin Presents first edition August 1982
ISBN 0-373-10525-8

Original hardcover edition published in 1982
by Mills & Boon Limited

CHAPTER ONE

HANNA had heard a lot about him, of course. She had even spoken to him briefly on the phone. But coming face to face with Ryan Donalson, the television director, was an experience she hoped would not have to be repeated often.

'Look here, Miss Whatever-your-name-is,' he said, 'it's no good Jessica sending messages. I want her here this afternoon at five-thirty for a top priority production meeting. She knows how important it is.'

The rudeness of the man! Hanna's eyes widened in surprise, because Jessica always sang his praises, warm affection evident even when she said he was in one of his difficult moods. She had understood they would marry one day, and it was for this reason she had come personally to Beauman Studios instead of phoning as Jessica had suggested. It had seemed kinder.

'If you'll let me finish explaining. . . .'

But the cold voice cut in. 'No excuses. Five-thirty, I said. There's been a schedule change and we're flying out to the States on Thursday. I'll need my script-writer on hand.'

'Oh, but she can't!' Hanna cried.

'What do you mean, can't. Just get back there and tell her.'

And Ryan Donalson strode back into the production control room without giving her a chance to say anything else. Hanna was angrier than she had been in years. He had spoken to her as if she was not worth a moment of his time, and surely there was nothing worse than starting a sentence with 'Look here'.

He certainly had no manners!

For the first time Hanna was glad that Jessica had married someone else. It had come as a great shock when she heard about it this morning, but now she decided it could only be for the best. How dreadful if she had married this arrogant, impossible man!

Jessica was a wonderful person, but even now, after being her secretary for six months, Hanna found her eccentricity the hardest thing to cope with. If she was working on a script that required background material she knew little about, Jessica would pack her bag and disappear without warning for days on end, leaving only a scribbled note of explanation. She bought clothes and discarded them on the slightest whim, ordered taxis and cancelled them because she forgot where she had been going. Yet her work was brilliant. So really it shouldn't have come as such a surprise that she had got married in the same erratic way.

'Darling,' she had said, as soon as Hanna got inside the door of the lovely mews house, 'I hoped you'd be early today. Guess what? I'm marrying Alistair Kerby at ten-thirty this morning! For goodness' sake come and help me get ready. There's a thousand and one things to be done and I'm too excited to do anything at all.'

Hanna thought she couldn't have heard right. 'Whenever was this decided? I thought you didn't know Alistair Kerby.'

'I didn't until Friday evening,' Jessica said.

'When I left you were about to phone him and complain about the "Women in Top Jobs" article. I remember you calling him names and saying he had no right to publish anything about you without an interview.'

Jessica smiled. 'That's right. He actually apologised and said would I have dinner with him to rectify the matter.' She paused, and the smile deepened as she lifted her shoulders and closed her lovely dark eyes. 'Oh, it was a marvellous evening!'

'It must have been,' said Hanna, with raised eyebrows.

'On Saturday we spent the day in Brighton. Yesterday I cooked lunch for us here and we went to church in the evening. Today we're getting married. He's the most wonderful thing that's ever happened to me. I decided to marry him the first moment I set eyes on him. Say you're happy for me.'

'Oh, Jessica!'

There was nothing else Hanna could say. She was a practical girl who considered carefully before doing anything, and the speed with which Jessica had arranged things was too much to take in all at once.

'You'll have to come to the register office with us, Hanna,' Jessica went on. 'I told Alistair you'd be a witness. Then when you get back here you'd better phone Ryan at the studios and explain. I had him on the phone at dawn this morning with some garbled message about a meeting today. Honestly, I wasn't paying proper attention. He'll be furious, but *you* can pacify him. I'm sorry, Hanna,' there was genuine concern in her eyes, 'I'm leaving you with an awful lot to do. You shouldn't be such a good secretary!'

They had gone into the bedroom where clothes were strewn across the bed and chairs, the wardrobe open, drawers overflowing. It was an elegant room, carpeted with thick cream pile which could just be seen through the scattered shoes, cases and handbags, and June sunshine brought the red and gold curtains to vivid life. The matching bedspread was hidden under dresses of all colours, and two glamorous negligées were draped over the brass bedhead rails.

'Tell me first what you want to take with you and I'll start packing,' said Hanna. 'I take it you're off on honeymoon straight after the ceremony.'

'To Rome, darling. Alistair has an assignment there tomorrow and we'll combine work with pleasure.'

Hanna began carefully folding some of the dresses

Jessica tossed in her direction and left them beside a case until heavier things had been stowed at the bottom.

'I hope that means you're taking the final episode of *The Forty-seven Days* to work on,' she said.

Jessica laughed. 'No, I'm not. I couldn't concentrate on the American Civil War while I'm among the Romans.' She held up a calf-length evening dress of sea green silk, studied it a second, then threw it down. 'I'll never wear that. Can't think why I bought it.'

'But what am I to say if Ryan Donalson asks about it?' said Hanna.

'He won't, darling. The script is finished. It's only an alteration he wants me to make, and they're not filming on location for weeks yet.' She stretched luxuriously. 'No, no work for me. As soon as Alistair gets through his job we're going on to Capri and I intend to do nothing but laze in the sun all day.'

The wedding was over so quickly Hanna could hardly believe it had taken place, and there were no celebrations afterwards, just champagne at the pub opposite the register office, then back to the house to collect Jessica's luggage which they had managed to confine to two suit-cases after a struggle, and then they were away. Alistair had said he didn't want any publicity.

'If anyone in my office had got wind of it there'd have been a flock of cameramen blocking the pavement,' he said. 'And knowing the boys they'd have insisted on standing us drinks until closing time. We'd never have got away.'

Hanna liked him. This disconcerted her because she had been prepared to dislike him on sight. He wrote a witty, often controversial column, and she had pictured him being a middle-aged philanderer with a sharp tongue and no taste in clothes. But he was none of these things. She liked his suede jacket and the blue shirt that matched his eyes, and he had an easy smile that made him disturbingly attractive. He looked younger than Jessica, who was thirty, and it was plain to see why she had been immediately enchanted. They made a striking pair, dark heads close as they signed the register, hand in hand coming out into the sunshine as man and wife, and when they looked at each other their love was there for the world to see. Alistair was one of those people who seem to have been a life-long friend after only a single meeting. Perhaps that was what made him such a good journalist.

It was a different world that Hanna moved in since she had started working for Jessica, and she was not yet used to a way of living where the unexpected was always round the next corner. Looking at things by this new standard she decided Ryan Donalson would probably accept the turn of events philosophically and shrug his shoulders. All the same, she felt sorry for him. He and Jessica had been close.

The house was strangely empty when Jessica and Alistair left. Hanna had been working there alone before when Jessica was away, but this time it didn't seem the same. She didn't feel at ease. It was still not midday, and twice she picked up the phone intending to ring Ryan Donalson, but it was such a callous way to give him the news and she wished Jessica had had the decency to tell him herself. Fond as she was of her, there were times when things were expected of Hanna that were more than a secretary's duties, and she began to wonder why she had given up a reasonably uncomplicated job with a publishing firm to work here instead.

Feeling in need of a break anyway, Hanna finally decided to take a taxi to Beauman Studios. And there her troubles had started all over again. First of all she had difficulty getting inside because she didn't have a pass, and only by mentioning Jessica Franklin's name had she managed to get as far as Reception, and it was sheer luck that the receptionist was new and thought she *was* Jessica Franklin that she was sent up to the production room. Obviously Jessica had been there often.

So now she stood outside the room with no idea what she was going to do next. It was no good going away until she had made the man listen, whether he wanted to or not. His script-writer had already flown off in a different direction to the States, and it was vital he know about it before the all-important meeting.

While she was trying to pluck up courage and march in after him, the door opened again and a blonde girl came out, tall and beautiful, but obviously harassed. An angry voice carried in her wake and she raised her eyes in exasperation when she saw Hanna.

'He's impossible today!' she declared.

No need to ask who she meant.

'I've got to speak to him again,' said Hanna. 'He wouldn't give me a chance to explain properly, and it's most important.'

The girl flicked her hair away from her neck as if the atmosphere had made her hot and uncomfortable, yet she still maintained an air of confidence which Hanna envied.

'Honey, unless it's a dire emergency I'd leave it till another day,' she advised. 'All his schedules have been altered, and if he doesn't calm down there won't be any staff left to work on them anyway.'

Hanna sighed. 'Well, I'm afraid what I have to tell him won't improve things. I'd better just wait.'

'Please yourself. Though I suppose if it's *really* important you'd better get it over with.' She gave a grin. 'Preferably while I'm downstairs on the floor! Good luck!'

When she had gone, Hanna took a deep breath. She was glad she had worn her favourite Indian cotton skirt and high-heeled sandals that morning. They at least had been reasonably suitable for a wedding before coffee time and a confrontation with an irate television director before lunch. All the girls she had seen here seemed to be wearing tight jeans and T-shirts, but she didn't feel too out of place, and she certainly wasn't going to be intimidated by a man who hadn't the courtesy to listen to what she had to say. A phone call would have been simpler after all, and as Ryan Donalson did not seem to possess any sensitivity it had just been a waste of time coming. She looked at the door, decided his temper could hardly get any worse, and went inside.

He was speaking into a microphone while monitor sets in front of him transmitted different views of the scene being filmed below. She recognised straight away that they were shooting part of *The Forty-seven Days*, and in spite of her apprehension she felt the first thrill of excitement. She had been working on the script with Jessica for weeks and was longing to see the words translated into visual drama.

'Lindsay, for God's sake get down on that floor and sort this lot out!' Ryan thundered. 'You ought to be down there by now. Hold it, will you?'

For a minute Hanna had been lost in the scene, which was set in one of the ante-bellum houses in Vicksburg, Mississippi, when the town was under siege. The acting had seemed superb, the atmosphere tense, but not half so tense apparently as the atmosphere in this small room. Was he picking faults for the sake of it, or was he genuinely not satisfied with the results he was getting? The production assistant and the vision mixer sat back in their seats, resigned. This, Hanna guessed, was one of the difficult moods Jessica dreaded.

'If you mean the person who just left, she'll be down in a minute,' said Hanna. 'Mr Donalson, I realise this is a bad time, but I *must* speak to you. If you'll tell me where to wait I don't mind, but there's something you must know.'

He looked round, said nothing. Then he leaned over the microphone and spoke in a more reasonable tone.

'Okay, break for lunch. I guess we all need it.'

He rubbed a hand across his eyes and stood up. The other two men exchanged a few words with him on some technical matter, then drifted out, and Hanna was alone in this confined space with the most unnerving man she had ever met. He was very tall, over six foot, which made her doubly glad of heels to give her height, for when he looked at her she needed all her self-confidence to stay calm. His shirt was open untidily at the neck and his tie was almost undone. If anything this man was how she had pictured Alistair would be, except that she could not imagine him philandering. Those smouldering good looks would ensure that he need never run after women. There were some who would undoubtedly come running if he so much as smiled, supposing that he *could* smile on occasions, and Hanna felt slightly disgusted at the thought of close contact with him. The feeling he had roused in her from the very first moment was good old-fashioned anger.

Then surprisingly he had the grace to apologise.

'Sorry, I wasn't very civil to you just now,' he said. 'Jessica should have been on the receiving end, not you. Now, what makes you think she won't be able to come to America? The arrangements are made and she knows darn well she has to be there.'

How long had he been dictating to Jessica in this way? Hanna's sympathies were reversed in a moment, and she was glad to be able to squash that arrogance.

'Jessica was married this morning,' she said. 'She's already left for Italy on her honeymoon.'

He was reaching for his jacket that was draped over the back of his chair, but froze momentarily. His expression did not appear to change, yet when he looked at her his eyes darkened and it was impossible to judge his reaction.

'Strange she didn't mention it when we had lunch on Friday,' he said, as if discussing a trivial matter. 'I presume it's someone I know.'

'I doubt if you do. She didn't know him herself until Friday.'

His unblinking gaze narrowed, as if he wanted to throw her out for daring to make such a ridiculous statement. 'You must be joking.'

'I assure you I'm not. It's Alistair Kerby, the colum-
nist . . .'

'. . . who wrote that Women in Top Jobs article.' His
body tensed and he looked away, awakened to the truth
and not liking it. 'Why the wretch practically slandered
her! Quote: 'Beautiful, high-minded Miss Franklin will
be holding her job for a very long time. She has been
known to say that marriage is for the mediocre and
those with time to make it work.' It wasn't easy to pacify
her when she showed it to me. Well, I hope she finds
time to make this insane arrangement work, but not at
my expense!'

He spoke coldly, but Hanna gave him the benefit of
the doubt and tried to believe there must be a softer
core to him somewhere that would be hurt by the news.

'They were very happy this morning,' she said gently.
'I think it was a case of love at first sight.'

'Spare me the details. I don't need them.' He wiped a
hand across his forehead where thick curly hair lay
damp. It was very hot. 'What's your name?'

'Hanna Ballantyne. I'm Jessica's secretary.'

'Yes,' he said, and looked at her again, but this time
as if he was seeing her as a person and not just an inter-
ruption in his overloaded schedule. 'Yes, I recognise
your voice. It's nice.'

Hanna felt her own face getting hot. There were no
windows in the room and she wondered how anyone
could breathe in there for long.

'Thank you,' she said.

He went on, 'Tell me, do *you* approve of this marriage?'

The question was unexpected, and it wasn't asked as if
he genuinely wanted her opinion. He was trying to find out
if he could make her an ally. Well, if he thought he could
use her as a tool against Jessica he was wrong! She knew
where her loyalties were, and whether she approved or not,
it was no concern of Ryan Donalson's.

'It's not up to me to say. I liked Mr Kerby, and I wish them every happiness,' she said.

'Hmm.'

The murmured acknowledgement could have meant anything. He was studying her, assessing her still, and she didn't like it. His next question swung the conversation so completely she was taken unawares.

'What do you know about Vicksburg, Mississippi, Hanna?'

'Quite a lot since working on the script with Jessica. She's been there, and she's done a lot of research.'

'With you helping her.'

'Yes, when I could,' said Hanna, wondering what he was leading to. 'I have an aunt who married an American and lives in Vicksburg, so I managed to get a lot of historical material through her.'

'Hmm,' he said again, thoughtfully. 'Interesting. You must tell me about her.'

'But there isn't anything to tell. She's very ordinary.'

He turned to pick up some papers, and it was a relief to be released from the scrutiny of those grey-brown eyes.

'I was only thinking it would be somewhere for you to stay when you go over there,' he said.

She smiled. 'I intend to go one day. I've been saving up and now air fares are cheaper . . .'

'You're going next Thursday, in place of Jessica.'

'What!' The exclamation burst from her.

'I've got to have someone on hand to do script alterations if necessary. You're capable of working on them without her, aren't you?'

'No,' she said, bemused. Then indignation gave a lift to her chin. 'I certainly wouldn't alter a single word of Jessica's scripts without her permission. And I've no intention of going anywhere next Thursday, Mr Donalson.'

'You'd better call me Ryan. It's Christian name terms around the studios.'

'But I've nothing to do with the studios.'

He drew his jacket off the back of the chair and slung it over one shoulder, using his index finger like a coat-hook.

'We'll discuss it this evening after the meeting,' he said, holding the door open and obviously expecting her to precede him into the corridor. 'I haven't time now. Can you be back here by seven?'

Hanna was amazed at the way he took things for granted. No question, it seemed, of her already having an engagement for the evening. He assumed she would drop everything and come running back for abrupt instructions he had no right to be giving. Well, bully for him! He'd picked the wrong one if he thought that was what she would do. She walked beside him down uncarpeted stairs, her heels clicking a staccato rhythm like a miniature war-dance.

'Mr Donalson, there's nothing to discuss. Much as I'd like to visit America, and thank you for the offer, I can't possibly go at a moment's notice. I have a job, you know.'

'And Jessica is under contract to the studios, which makes you indirectly affected. So I'd appreciate a talk with you after the meeting—Miss Ballantyne.'

There was no mistaking the sarcasm in his tone, and Hanna was tingling with the urge to make another scathing refusal, but he was, after all, one of the top men in television, gifted, always in demand to make programmes that were guaranteed money-spinners. Not that that gave him licence to walk over people, but it gave him authority and for Jessica's sake she could see it would be wiser to acquiesce.

'I came by taxi this morning,' she said.

'Then by all means come by taxi this evening and charge it up to expenses.'

'Thank you, but I prefer to be independent.'

They had reached a side door leading out to the road and he stopped, opening it.

'As you wish,' he said. 'I'm afraid I can't lay on a chauffeur-driven limousine to pick you up, but no doubt you'll find some way of getting here.'

She was about to make another sharp retort, but he stood aside for her to pass, and as she did so she glanced up and saw that he was smiling. Yes, he really could smile, and the effect was devastating. Hanna's heart did a peculiar somersault because she was quite unprepared for the change of tactics, and for some reason she was even more annoyed.

'Should I come to the main entrance, or would you rather let me in through this side door?' she asked tartly.

'Miss Ballantyne, I've made a note that there's a touch of red in your hair,' he said, and the smile reached his voice. 'I'll leave word at the gate that you're expected.'

She went out into the road.

'By the way,' he added, 'thank you for coming personally with the news. Jessica hadn't even the guts to tell me on the phone this morning.'

A moment later the door was shut and Hanna was alone. She found she was in a side street and was not sure of her direction. Not sure of anything at all. Since dawn this morning everything had changed, and it looked as if it was never going to be the same again.

CHAPTER TWO

HANNA spent the rest of the day in a state of agitation. Her encounter with Ryan Donalson had left her feeling as if she had been buffeted in a storm, and she was certain the storm was not yet over. All she could do was use the lull to re-form her thoughts. Nothing had prepared her for the impact of such an objectionable man, and when Jessica returned it was to be hoped she could explain how she had managed to give the impression that he was an easygoing type who could be dangled on a string until needed. How had she put up with him for so long?

He had no right to make any demands on her time. Hanna stood very straight in the middle of Jessica's office, feet planted firmly on the carpet as she mentally stood her ground. Jessica was her employer. On no account would she do anything that would not meet with her approval. It was quite plain he thought he was going to persuade her to change her mind and go to the States with him, but it was quite out of the question. Quite out of the question. She repeated the words out loud to give them weight.

There was plenty of work that needed her attention, and Hanna made a determined effort to get on with it after a late, half-hearted lunch, but the notes were a meaningless blur and after the second attempt to make sense of them she put the papers away in the drawer of the rosewood desk. Tomorrow was another day and she would make a fresh start when she had regained her composure.

She had no idea how long Jessica was going to be away. It would depend how long Alistair could be spared from the newspaper, of course, but it sounded as though they meant to spend as long as possible in Capri. Everything was so uncertain that Hanna felt ill at ease, and she wished there was someone she could talk to in the house. Mrs Smart, the woman who came daily to clean, had been given an unexpected day off, and with no one around even a cat would have been company, but there was nothing except the ticking of the mantelpiece clock. And it was going to be like this for days. Jessica hadn't had time to leave any specific instructions about work, so once the research notes were typed there was little else she could do.

Hanna wandered over to the window and looked out at the colourful flower tubs across the way, bright with fuchsias, petunias and trailing lobelia. One of the things she disliked most about living in the city was not having a garden, and she thought nostalgically about her home down in Kernsmere where her mother was sure to be busy weeding the borders if the weather was fine. It was good to think about Kernsmere. It gave her a peaceful feeling that soothed the irritations of the day, and she longed to be walking down the village street that she had known since childhood, exchanging greetings with old friends.

Perhaps Jessica wouldn't mind if she took a week's leave instead of hanging around wasting time. After all, she had been working for six months without a break, so she was entitled to a holiday. The thought cheered her up straight away, and before she could look for reasons why it wasn't possible, she decided to phone her parents. They were always asking when she going home to see them, but she had put off making the journey while things were going so well in town. Not that there was anything wrong now, but it would be nice to be cosseted for a few days.

And there was another reason. She needed an excuse to give Ryan Donalson if he suggested again that she ought to be on location with the television crew. If she had plans ready made he wouldn't be able to insist. She had been going over in her mind what she was going to say to him, but pulled herself up sharply. Anyone would think she was afraid of him. Well, she most definitely wasn't, and she would stand her ground no matter what argument he put up.

She dialled her parents' number and waited rather longer than usual for an answer so as to give her mother time to come up from the garden.

'Don't tell me, you were picking sweet peas,' she said, as soon as she heard her mother's voice.

'Hanna darling, how lovely!' There was no mistaking the pleasure in her tone. 'I was thinking of ringing you this evening.'

'How would you like to see me tomorrow instead?' asked Hanna.

'Oh, that would be wonderful! Your father *will* be pleased. He keeps saying how much he misses you. What time will you come?'

They talked for several minutes, making plans and exchanging bits of news that could be enlarged upon when they were together, and Hanna felt the pull of home getting stronger by the minute. Strange, then, that just before she put the phone down she asked a quite irrelevant question.

'Mother, what's Aunt Rachael like?'

There was a pause at the other end of the line while her mother thought a moment. Then: 'Darling, I haven't seen her for twenty years. She's got fat and middle-aged by her photos, but I'll bet she hasn't changed much from the happy girl she used to be. Can't you tell by her letters?'

'Yes, she sounds fun.'

'Why did you want to know?' her mother asked.

Hanna smiled. 'It's just that I could have been going to see her at the weekend, but I'd rather see *you* instead.'

'Hanna!'

'I'll tell you about it later.'

After she put the phone down, Aunt Rachael was still uppermost in her mind. Over the past few months she had heard frequently from her mother's sister and found her a lively correspondent, thrilled to be asked to help with information for a television series. And Vicksburg sounded a fascinating place, right on the Mississippi River, steeped in its Civil War history, and famed for Bourbon pie and mint juleps. Hanna had always wanted to visit the Deep South, and Aunt Rachael was begging her to come at the first opportunity. So why was she so adamant about refusing to go now she had the chance? Loyalty to Jessica was a very sound reason, but under the circumstances she hardly thought she would lose her job if Ryan Donalson really put the pressure on. Jessica knew full well how demanding he could be. No, the truth was she would never be able to tolerate the man if she had to be in his company for any length of time.

But she was committed to seeing him this evening, and had to allow at least half an hour to get across to Beauman Studios. There was no point in going back to her own flat first. For one thing it was in the opposite direction, and apart from perhaps changing into something a bit smarter there was nothing she needed to go there for. It would be a waste of time and bus fare. It wouldn't matter if she was still wearing the same clothes. Most likely it would only take a few minutes to say whatever he had to say, and a phone call would have been quite sufficient. It was inconsiderate, to say the least, but he was the sort who expected people to drop everything and come running if he so much as beckoned.

With time still to spare, she decided to tidy Jessica's bedroom which had been left in a state of chaos after the cases were packed. It wasn't fair to leave it to Mrs Smart tomorrow, and Hanna felt that Jessica might prefer her secretary to her daily woman putting things away for her.

Hanna had never had occasion to go into the bed-

room until today, and as she went in for the second
time late afternoon sun was shining on a round table by
the window. It was covered by a circular cloth of cream
damask with a red and gold fringe that touched the
floor, and on it was a coloured photograph in a silver
frame of Ryan Donalson. Her eyes were drawn to it, yet
she hadn't even noticed it was there before. Her im-
mediate thought was that when Jessica came home with
her husband it would be embarrassing if another man's
photograph was still in her bedroom, and Hanna
thought the wisest thing was to put it away somewhere.

It was a very good photograph. She studied it a few
minutes, remembering the hypnotic effect of those grey-
brown eyes under craggy brows, and the determined set
of his chin. It was a strong face, made more dominant if
anything by the curly brown hair that framed it. She
could imagine her mother saying it was time his hair
saw a pair of scissors, but a smattering of grey among
the curls lent a sort of respectability, and the firm line
of his mouth showed he would not brook any criticism.
Every line of that handsome face spoke of ruthless
ambition, and she shuddered, wishing the evening was
over and she would not have to see him again.

There was a shallow drawer in the little bedside
table which seemed the best place and she pulled it
open, intending to lay the frame face downwards and
leave it there. But it was not so easy. The drawer was
full of letters, and the top sheet of paper with bold
handwriting couldn't be ignored. It wasn't that she
wanted to know what it said, but the words were
committed to memory before she even realised she had
read them.

'There's no one like you,' it said. 'So please, darling,
wait a bit longer before coming to a decision. Let's at
least discuss it like civilised people. You know how I
feel. Yours, Ryan.'

She hurriedly closed the drawer, as if someone had

come up behind her and caught her snooping, and went over to the dressing table, shutting the photograph among a pile of underclothes instead. She didn't want Jessica to think she had been prying. And she wished she hadn't seen the letter. The relationship between Jessica and Ryan had been nothing to do with her. It was no more than a vague background to her employer's private life, and she had only concerned herself with it this morning because she had been asked. But now she felt personally involved in some way. It was clear that Ryan loved Jessica, and no matter how much she disliked him she couldn't help a wave of sympathy stealing over her. It must be dreadful to love someone who didn't feel the same way, and she could guess what it had cost him to beg for another chance, all to no avail as it turned out.

Feeling more kindly disposed towards him, she wished that after all she'd made the journey over to her flat and changed. A T-shirt and cotton skirt were hardly the thing for evening, even if it was only for a brief meeting, but it was too late now to do anything about it. She started putting the rest of Jessica's dresses on hangers, trying to make room for them on the overcrowded rails in the wardrobe, and the last one she picked up off the floor was the sea-green silk that had been discarded earlier. It was a beautiful dress, not only for evenings, and Hanna held it against her, judging the effect in a long oval mirror. The colour suited her. It emphasised the green of her eyes, and brought out the copper tones in her hair. She put it on a hanger, loving the feel of the beautiful material, then on impulse she tried it on. It fitted perfectly.

Jessica would never know if she borrowed it for the evening. She had said she would never wear it herself and would probably give it away when she came back from honeymoon, so what harm was there in making use of it? Her black velvet jacket looked almost shabby over it, but it would have to do. She arranged the collar over the lapels, pulled the belt in another notch round her slim waist, and decided she now had enough confidence to face the dreaded Ryan Donalson in his den.

No problem getting into the studios this time. At reception the girl smiled and invited her to take a seat, apologising that the meeting was still in progress. Hanna went over to the window, away from a group of people who were queueing to get in to see a live show. Minutes passed and the crowd increased, hemming her in. Quarter past seven. Half past seven, and she was wondering just how much longer he intended keeping her waiting when a loud voice carried across the room.

'Miss Ballantyne! Mr Donalson will be with you shortly.'

All heads turned to see who was being addressed, and she felt too embarrassed to move. Anyone would think she was applying for a job as office junior! Then, afraid the call might be repeated, she threaded her way to the desk, temper giving her an unusually superior air.

'*I'm* Miss Ballantyne,' she said. 'Will someone kindly take me to Mr Donalson's office? I've waited long enough.'

The reception staff looked at each other, as though they couldn't believe their ears. Was everyone round here frightened of the man? There was a strange hush before someone condescended to do as she asked.

'Come this way, please,' one of the girls said.

She led Hanna through double doors and down a corridor towards the back of the building, past a studio where preparations were going on for the programme that was soon to be televised, and round a corner where it was quieter. She stopped at a door marked Private, knocked, and opened it.

'Miss Ballantyne,' she announced, and made a hasty retreat.

Hanna stood in the doorway. The room was plainly furnished in sober browns, but one wall was covered with posters from major productions and there seemed to be books and papers everywhere. She took these in at a glance, but her attention was riveted to the corner where there was a handbasin, because that was where Ryan was standing stripped to the waist and covered in soap suds.

'Don't stand there,' he shouted. 'Come in.'

She went inside and closed the door behind her. 'I'm sorry, I should have waited . . .'

'I'm sure you've seen people wash before,' he said, still with his back to her. 'This is as far as I'm going at the moment, if that's what's worrying you.'

Her face coloured. He rinsed off the soap and began towelling himself dry with great vigour, then he turned to speak. A gold medallion gleamed where there was dark hair on his chest, and his shoulders seemed broader than ever. He smiled, enjoying her discomfort.

'As it's getting late, Mr Donalson, I thought you would be glad to get whatever business you have with me over so that you can get home.'

'I take it you're in a hurry.' He was appraising the green dress, and she held her breath for fear he was going to say he had seen it before on Jessica. 'Is someone coming here to collect you?'

'No,' she said, wishing the answer could have been yes. 'I'm not going anywhere.'

He raised one eyebrow. 'In that case you can have dinner with me.'

He opened a cupboard by the sink unit. It seemed to serve as a wardrobe and he pulled out a brown shirt, thrusting his arms into it.

'I can't do that,' Hanna protested.

'Why not? I've a lot of things to talk over with you, and I'm too hungry to hang around here. Have you eaten yet this evening?'

'No—o.'

'That's settled, then.'

He buttoned the shirt and tucked it into his trousers,

found a tie that toned and knotted it swiftly. She watched, fascinated. He was one for making instant decisions, and she felt she wanted to clutch on to something to stop herself being swept along on the tide of this forceful personality. She was *not* going to let him dictate to her!

'I'm sure I can save you the trouble of taking me out,' she said, 'because if it's the trip to America you want to talk about, I repeat, I'm not going.'

He brushed his hair into some semblance of order. 'Let's just say I need company.'

There was no answer to that. Of course he would be feeling upset about Jessica, and eating alone would be a miserable affair. She ought to have realised.

'Well, as long as you know you can't change my mind about anything connected with Jessica's work. I've thought seriously about it all the afternoon, and I'm quite sure she wouldn't approve of me going anywhere with her scripts.'

'What do you fancy for dinner?' he asked, completely ignoring her words. 'Steak? Rainbow trout? Chicken in one of its various disguises?'

'A salad will do very nicely, thank you.'

He put on his jacket and went over to the window, lifting two slats of the venetian blinds with thumb and forefinger so that he could see out. The summer evening was marred by heavy cloud and a wind was getting up.

'I don't bring my car to the studios,' he said. 'Haven't you got a coat?'

Hanna thought of the shabby velvet jacket she had left on Jessica's bed after all because it had spoilt the effect of the dress, and determined not to let him know she regretted putting pride before comfort. She hadn't expected to be out long.

She said: 'I'm quite warm enough without one.'

'Silly girl. Never go without a coat in this wretched climate.'

'I don't think it's wretched. At least we don't have

earthquakes, droughts, hurricanes, you name it.'

She was conscious of arguing for the sake of it, and couldn't understand herself. The amused, slightly patronising tone of his voice aggravated so much that she wanted to automatically disagree with everything he said.

'Perhaps, as you haven't anything warm to wear, we'd better take a taxi,' he was saying.

'I'm not cold, Mr Donalson, but if *you* prefer to take a taxi, please say so.'

His hands were in his pockets, and he looked at her again with those penetrating eyes, as if he would like to cut her down to size. Obviously he was so used to people being in awe of him he resented any contradiction.

'On second thoughts, it might be as well to go to the Gambria,' he said.

One up to her. She smiled at the small victory, surprised at herself because it wasn't usually the way she behaved, but there was something about him that put her continually on the defensive.

Then she realised where he had said he would take her, and gasped.

'The Gambria? In Beau Square?' It was the haunt of millionaires and celebrities.

'Where else? I can hardly take you to the nearest Chinese takeaway in that dress.'

He put a hand beneath her elbow and turned her towards the door. The brief contact sent a shiver through her, and she moved away as quickly as she could. If she had known what problems Jessica's dress was going to cause she wouldn't have been in such a hurry to try it on.

All the same, as she walked up the steps to the main entrance of the Hotel Gambria, she couldn't help feeling excited. It was only a short distance from Beauman Studios and they had walked, but she almost wished she had arrived by car so that she could have the added thrill of having a uniformed doorman open the door for her.

'We'll go down to the Grill Room,' said Ryan. 'I'll introduce you to the finest steak you've ever tasted.'

As they went down the thickly carpeted stairs they were confronted by pink-tinted mirrors that did the most flattering things with their reflections, and the sight of herself beside Ryan Donalson made Hanna catch her breath, for he really was very good-looking. And he was known in the Grill Room, where a table was found in a pleasant alcove even though the place was full.

'We're busy this evening, Mr Donalson,' the head waiter said, 'but we shan't keep you waiting long.'

'We're not in a hurry,' said Ryan. 'Are we, Hanna?'

'No.' She was trying to act as if she frequented such luxurious restaurants every week of her life, and hoped he wouldn't guess how gauche she felt. She straightened her shoulders, and didn't make the mistake of looking round to see who was at the other tables. In fact she was feeling quite pleased with her air of composure when he shattered it with a single remark.

'Hanna Ballantyne, relax! I can't see your name on the menu.'

'I don't understand.'

'I mean I'm not going to eat you,' he said, 'even though you look very delectable.'

She was used to compliments within her own circle of acquaintances, but there was mockery in Ryan Donalson's tone and she hated him for it. He was making fun of her.

'Perhaps we could get down to discussing business,' she said coldly.

'By all means.' He sat back in his seat, still with his eyes on her, but she refused to be daunted and returned the chilling gaze. 'I want to know what you can tell me about Vicksburg.'

She was surprised. She thought the main reason he wanted to see her was so that he could hear more about Jessica's marriage. But perhaps it was too painful to talk about.

'What is it you want to know? Jessica has all the history books I managed to get about the siege and the battlefields. There are some brochures about the ante-bellum houses, and a few maps.'

'And the research department has done its own job thoroughly, too. No, I want to know about modern Vicksburg, and your family there.'

'Will you contact them?'

'I might.'

Hanna smiled at last, and her finely moulded cheek-bones showed to the best advantage when the corners of her mouth lifted. It was a sweet smile, lighting her eyes and giving warmth to her face.

'It's my mother's sister who lives there,' she said. 'They have a house on the outskirts and she says the magnolia trees are absolutely beautiful. I think it must be hilly, and you can go on riverboat trips on the Mississippi.'

'Has your aunt any family?' Ryan asked.

'She's a widow. Uncle Jake died years ago, but she has two sons, Jay and Leigh.'

'Your cousins.'

'Yes.' She related tales about them that Aunt Rachael had put in her letters, and by the time the steaks arrived she was much more at ease.

'Aunt Rachael has sent recipes I long to try. She makes gumbo and jumbalaya, and she says Leigh reckons her pecan pie is the best he's ever tasted. I'll give you her address.'

'There's no need,' he said. 'You can *take* me to meet them. I'll look forward to it.'

The devious wretch! He had deliberately encouraged her to talk about her American relations so that she would feel the pull of family ties, but she wasn't going to fall for that one either.

'For the last time, she told him. 'I am *not* going to the States. I've already decided to take the rest of this week as holiday, and I've told my mother I shall be going home to Kernsmere tomorrow.'

He tackled his steak with enjoyment, saying nothing for a moment, and she was afraid she had been too abrupt. After all, it would be an expenses paid trip, presumably, and he would think she ought to jump at the chance.

'I haven't seen my parents for six months,' she went on hesitantly, wanting to explain.

'That's all right,' he said. He put down his knife and fork. 'You can go down there tomorrow, and come back on Wednesday in time to do your packing. Take enough with you for two weeks, mostly cotton stuff. It's very hot in Mississippi at this time of the year.'

Hanna was speechless. He had more nerve than anyone she had ever met, and the thought of him giving orders like that for two days, never mind two weeks, was more than she could stand. She looked at his handsome, aggressive face and wondered how he could inspire tenderness in anybody. He was so sure of himself, so full of his own importance that no one else counted. Yet his voice was quiet now, not forceful as it had been when he was angry this morning, and the soft tone was appealing. Easy to be swayed by that low, almost seductive voice, and she closed her ears to its charm. He didn't impress her at all.

'What makes you think you can change my mind?' she challenged him.

He put one elbow on the table, hand beneath his chin, and studied her. 'I've two choices. Either I persuade *you* to come with me and make the best of it—I've *got* to have someone who knows the scripts well enough to make necessary alterations . . .'

He paused, perhaps waiting for Hanna to protest again, but she was anxious to know the second choice before commenting.

'Or . . .' she prompted.

'Or I sue Jessica for breach of contract and steer clear

of her scripts in future. There's no room for unreliable people in this business.'

'You can't do that!' she gasped.

'I can . . . and I will.'

She stared at him, hardly believing what she heard.

'But that's blackmail!' She stood up, pushing her plate away. 'How dare you put me in such a terrible position? I think you're despicable!'

She picked up her handbag and fled from the Grill Room, oblivious to the curious glances from people around. She wouldn't stay another minute in his company and listen to such heartless talk. All right, so he was feeling bad about Jessica and wanted revenge, but let him wait and sort it out with her instead of involving someone who had nothing to do with either of their personal problems.

She no longer saw the splendour of the Gambria foyer. All she wanted to do was get away, and she refused the doorman's offer to get a taxi because it wouldn't do to stand and wait until one came. That devil of a man would catch up with her, and she didn't want that. Instead, she crossed Beau Square and ran down a side street, not stopping until she came to the next main thoroughfare.

It was dark now and the street lights were on, but there were no shops to give extra illumination and the tall buildings in blackness surrounding her had a sinister feel about them. She didn't know how far it was to the nearest underground station, and couldn't see a bus stop, so she stood on the edge of the kerb, praying that a taxi would come along quickly.

She didn't see the youth who had followed her up the side street. It was a prickling sensation, a premonition of approaching danger that made her turn just as he sprang from the darkness to make a grab for her handbag, and as she jerked her arm sideways he missed his chance. Not daring to try again, he shot back into the shadows to escape the way he had come, but he had reckoned without the big man who had witnessed what happened as he also came up the side street. He caught hold of the youth and struggled with him, but it was too dark to see who was the stronger.

Hanna wanted to scream, but no sound came, and there was no one else around to come and give assistance. So she used the only weapon she had, the handbag which had been the cause of the trouble, intending to strike the youth on the arm so that he would lose his grip. But the bag swung higher than she meant it to, and caught the man on the side of his head. He reeled a second, and the boy took advantage of the unexpected respite to free himself from the man's grasp, fleeing down the dark street to hide and lick his wounds and prepare for his next victim.

The big man came into the light, covering his left eye with his hand.

'For God's sake, what do you carry around in that handbag?' he demanded. 'A house brick?'

She was trembling with shock, but went towards him to apologise and thank him for what he had done. Then, to her horror, she saw that it was Ryan Donalson.

CHAPTER THREE

HANNA woke up with cramp in her feet. She rubbed them hard and gingerly stretched her legs, rotating each numb ankle to restore the circulation. A blue tartan rug fell to the floor as she sat up on the studio couch, and as she leaned forward to pick it up she could see the reflection of Ryan Donaldson's bedroom in a long wall mirror. He hadn't moved since eleven o'clock last night, ten hours ago. She looked at her watch, flicked her wrist and looked again to make sure it was the right time.

It took a few minutes to recall all that had happened, and she went back over the evening, building up to that dreadful moment when she had struck a savage blow to Ryan's temple. If she had been going to toss a caber in the Highland Games she couldn't have put more force behind it, and she always kept a heavy torch in her bag in case it was dark when she returned to her flat, or she was attacked on the way. Such a blow would have felled a lesser man. Ryan had managed to keep on his feet, but his abuse must have been heard as far back as Beauman Studios, and all she could do was apologise, until she saw the swelling that was closing his left eye as she watched it.

'We'll have to get you to the nearest Casualty Department,' she said, common sense overriding the initial shock at what she had done. 'You might have concussion.'

'I am *not* going to any hospital!' He towered above her, a menacing figure in his anger, and ice-cold shivers flowed through her.

'But your eye ...'

'... is a fine sight, thanks to you. I'll put something

34

on it when I get home.'

Hanna bit her lip, so full of contrition she could have burst into tears. But the humour of the situation came to her rescue and an irrepressible giggle escaped her like a hiccough.

'Perhaps if we went back to the Gambria they'd find a raw steak for you to put on it,' she said.

'As I tore out without paying anyway, they'd probably take one look at me and send for the police.'

And in spite of the pain, his mouth, too, turned up at the corners in a wry smile. It was a sort of truce, but lasted so short a time it was barely noticeable. A taxi came into view and he signalled it, taking a firm grip on her arm as if he thought she would try to get away.

'Where do you live? I'll put you in this one and wait for the next to come along,' he said, as the cab drew up.

'Oh, no, you don't,' she protested. 'I'm coming with you to make sure you get some treatment for that eye.'

'I don't need treatment.'

'Either the hospital, or your place where I can call a doctor.'

Ryan was about to let forth in his usual volatile manner when the taxi driver put his head out of the window and joined in.

'Better do as she says, guv'nor,' he said. 'Whoever slugged you made a right good job of it.'

'You should see the other chap,' said Hanna quickly.

No one ever told Ryan Donalson what to do and she fully expected another outburst, but to her surprise he merely taunted her.

'You invite yourself to my flat at your own risk,' he said. 'I take no responsibility.'

He bundled her in, giving an address to the driver which she couldn't hear, and the door slammed shut. She moved to the farthest corner, sensing the mockery in his expression, and she hoped her heartbeats were not as loud as they sounded in her own ears. It would never do for him to know she was nervous. Close proximity to him in the darkness of the taxi brought a tingling sensation to her skin and when she stole a glance in his direction her pulses quickened. Whatever had possessed her to suggest going anywhere with this unpredictable stranger who antagonised her with every word? His profile, seen in silhouette, was like that of a Greek god and his opinion of himself matched it. His last remark implied that she had an ulterior motive in wanting to go home with him, but if he thought she was throwing herself at him he couldn't be more wrong. She would leave that for women with a taste for male chauvinism in its most blatant form.

His flat was in a Victorian block called River Mansions. The name was written in gold in an old-fashioned skylight above the main entrance, and she followed him up to the first floor. It was luxurious. The hall was as big as a lounge and obviously served as an extra room, while all the other rooms opened off it. He switched on the light. The walls were the palest silver grey and grey cushions of various sizes were heaped on a navy-blue suite which looked made for comfort. But what gave the room beauty was the lower part of the walls, which was patterned with blue and white Delft tiles. Any other time she would have stopped to admire and exclaim, but now there was more urgent business. There was a telephone on a table beside the couch and she went straight over to it, her feet sinking into the pile of the dark grey carpet.

'Right,' she said, 'what's your doctor's number?'

He came up behind her and took the receiver from her hand, putting it back on the rest. 'I don't need a doctor.'

'Mr Donalson, you need somebody.'

'You'll do, Miss Ballantyne.' He was so close she could smell the after-shave he used, feel his breath against her hair and the brush of his sleeve against her bare arm. She daren't move for fear he would touch her, and every muscle in her body was tense. If she had turned round she would have been practically in his arms, so she stayed still and after a moment he took a step backwards. 'What I mean is you'll find cotton wool, lint, antiseptic and anything else you may need in the bathroom cabinet. I'm sure you're capable of cleaning up the wounds you inflicted.'

The sarcasm in his voice was infuriating and he was doing his best to make her feel the need to do penance. She hated him and would have given anything to be back in her own flat, as far away from him as possible, but one look at the swollen, discoloured eye reminded her that it was her duty to see he had proper attention.

'Antiseptic and cotton wool are not enough,' she said. 'Concussion can have a delayed effect and you might lose consciousness from internal bleeding. You shouldn't take risks with a head injury.'

He put his head back and roared with laughter. 'Miss Know-it-all, it was my eye that got in your way, not my brain. Don't dramatise—that's my job.'

She faced him defiantly, temper drawing her mouth into a prim line, then she swung past him.

'Goodnight, Mr Donalson.'

But he was too quick for her. His hand shot out, grasping her wrist as she passed, and she couldn't escape.

'Where do you think you're going, Hanna?'

'Home—where else do you think?'

'I think you're going to stay here. It's getting late and you're not safe to be out alone.'

She tried to shake off the restraining hand, but he was too strong for her.

'I'd feel safer in Piccadilly Circus than here with you,' she said. 'Please let me go.'

He pulled her closer bending her arm so that her hand was against his chest and she could feel the warmth of his body through the fine material of his shirt. He was trying to impress her with his strength, his air of authority, but she was not going to be intimidated. She met his eyes, unflinching, and tried to ignore the burning sensation in her wrist.

'Tell me,' he said, 'how did Jessica manage to get such an impulsive, self-willed, organising woman for a secretary?'

'I worked for the firm who publish her books,' said Hanna. 'I wanted to change my job and she needed a new secretary.'

'And do you order her life the way you're trying to do mine? I doubt it. No one will ever get Jessica out of her dizzy ways.'

'I take it you tried and failed.'

As soon as the words were out she regretted them. He dropped her hand and gave her a slight push to widen the distance between them. There were more ways than one of hurting him, and she guessed the latter was more painful than the physical blow had been.

'I'm sorry . . .' she began. She hadn't met this man until this morning, yet they were sparring like enemies. She couldn't understand it.

He ignored her apology and went across the hall, opening one of the doors. It led to a bedroom.

'Tell you what,' he said, 'we'll compromise. No doctor, but you can stay the night, and if it looks like I'm drifting into a state of unconsciousness you can call him then.'

His face was serious, but there was no mistaking the mockery in his tone, and she was furious.

'You must think I'm mad!'

'On the contrary, your concern for my welfare does you credit. I'm sure you wouldn't want me to stay here alone in my present state of health, so I'll get out some extra pillows and some blankets for the couch.'

'But there's no need to do that,' she said.

'Why not? You'll be cold out here without them.'

He went into the bedroom and she pressed her fingers to her temples, wondering if she would wake in a minute from a bad dream. Never before had she been in such an impossible situation. When Ryan came back to the doorway he had taken off his jacket and tie.

'I won't stay here in your flat all night. How dare you suggest it!' she stormed. 'Please phone for a taxi for me at once.'

'Miss Ballantyne, don't tell me you have old-fashioned scruples,' he drawled. 'I assure you I'm quite harmless.'

'I'm not stopping to find out.'

He was leaning against the doorpost, studying her with a half smile on his lips, but as she started to turn away he put his hand to his head, closed his eyes, and began slipping gently down towards the floor.

'Oh, no!' she gasped, and ran towards him in panic. 'I warned you this might happen.'

As she reached him he was slowly straightening up again and the smile deepened.

'You can't leave me, Hanna,' he said. The amusement he found in the charade was exasperating. 'If anything happened to me you'd never forgive yourself. How can you possibly let me spend the night alone?'

He was trapping her. The indolent way he leaned in the doorway with arms folded and a self-complacent expression made her temper flare, but she knew she must keep it in check. She was enduring the consequences of having struck him once and had to resist the urge to do it a second time no matter how much he provoked her. But there was no need to suffer his insolence in silence.

'I can quite easily,' she said. 'It seems you want to substitute me for Jessica in more ways than one. Well, if all you want is a woman for the night, you've got the wrong one. I don't go in for that sort of thing!'

The angry words were out before she could stop them and they struck with the accuracy of a poison dart. The danger she had seen behind his smile was nothing to the ominous narrowing of his eyes at her outburst. His brows came together, lowering with anger, and there was a threatening pause.

'You surprise me,' he said at last, his voice quiet and heavy with ridicule. 'The way you insisted on coming to my flat gave me quite the opposite impression.'

He was not playing any more. He stretched out his arm and gripped her by the shoulder, the sudden movement as lithe as a tiger pouncing on its prey, and he swung her round.

'You know that wasn't what I meant,' she protested in alarm.

He was looking down at her with fire in his eyes. 'I don't know anything about you. We're strangers, you and I, so don't presume to know anything about me either.'

It was a warning firmly given, and Hanna lifted her chin and straightened her back as if preparing for an onslaught. The onslaught came, but not in the manner she had expected, and her rigid body almost snapped when he pulled her roughly against him. His mouth came down hard on hers, bruising her lips with the force he used to part them, and she had no breath to cry out. She managed to use her hands and fought him furiously, but he was too strong for her. She moved her head from side to side in a desperate effort to free her mouth from the brutal pressure, but until he decided it was enough she was captive and his hands tangled her hair as he tried to hold her still. In another moment she would have used her knee to give a damaging blow in self-defence, yet even as she struggled she was not afraid of him, and when he let go abruptly it was rage that made her gasp for breath.

'You unspeakable creature!' she yelled. 'Just let me get out of here. I don't ever want to see you again!'

She ran from him once more, aware that he was rubbing his lip where she had tried to bite him. He made no attempt to stop her.

'Never talk to me that way about Jessica,' he said, his voice hardly raised. 'There's no comparison between you.'

Hanna turned as she lifted the latch on the door and he was still standing on the same spot, legs astride. The smile had returned. She slammed out of the flat, hating him so much she couldn't trust herself to say another word.

When she got down to the main entrance fear caught up with her. Not fear of Ryan Donalson. The battle with him had left her with a strange kind of exhilaration that gave an edge to every move she made, and she stood for a moment on the top step to take a gulp of fresh air. It was then that a storm which had been threatening all day chose to break overhead with a vivid flash of lightning, illuminating the road and followed almost immediately by a crack of thunder so loud that she covered her head with her arms, for Hanna was terrified of storms. Rain began to fall, huge drops spattering at her feet, and in seconds there was a downpour. Even if she had had a coat she would have been soaked in no time. Another flash of lightning was more than she could stand and she dashed back inside the door, trembling from head to foot.

There was no knowing how long it would last, and she had to make a snap decision whether to brave the elements or Ryan Donalson. It didn't take much doing. Anything was preferable to being out in a thunderstorm. She went slowly back up the linoleum-covered stairs to his door and hesitated outside, her finger hovering over the bell-push while she wondered whether perhaps she could sit out on the landing until it was over. Only then it would be too late to get home on her own.

She was still trying to pluck up courage to press the bell when the door opened so unexpectedly she almost fell inside, and Ryan was staring at her, equally surprised.

'There's a dreadful storm,' she said meekly.

'I know. I heard the rain and was going to see how far you'd got without a coat. You'd better come back in.'

'Thank you.' She stood in the hall, uncertain where to go because he walked off and left her without another word. Thunder rolled again overhead and she tried to ignore it. Then she heard sounds from what she took to be the kitchen over on the right and went to find him. A kettle had just boiled and he was pouring water into a basin. Cotton wool and a bottle of antiseptic lotion were already on the table.

'Would you like me to do that for you?' she asked.

'If you like.' His sleeves were rolled up and he tested the heat of the water before trusting her with it, then sat himself on an upright chair.

She wished he would yell when she bathed his eye, but he didn't. He sat there with great composure and looked as if he quite enjoyed the attention. She worked gently and finding no skin broken she got some ice cubes from the refrigerator and applied cold compresses. Neither of them spoke. When she eased the thick hair away from his temple curling strands caught like tendrils round her fingers, and not a flinch disturbed the hard, masculine planes of his face. Afterwards he prescribed himself a brandy, but she declined the curt invitation to join him. Coffee would have been better, only she wasn't going to ask for anything.

The rain had eased, but the lights still flickered intermittently and the thunder had hardly lessened at all.

'I've always been frightened of storms,' she said when yet another clap made her cover her ears instinctively.

'There had to be a reason for that white face. If it had been me you wouldn't have come back up here.'

Colour returned to her cheeks. 'Perhaps you won't mind if I spend the night on your couch after all.'

'It's your decision,' he shrugged, as if he didn't care one way or the other. 'You can have the bed. I'll stay out here. And you needn't be afraid—I'm not going to attack you.'

He made it sound insulting and she wanted to send a stinging retort, but that would have been asking for trouble, so she contented herself with marching into the bedroom to collect the blanket and pillow he had offered before.

'I prefer to sleep on the couch, if it's all the same to you.'

'Please yourself. It's too late to argue.'

He went into the bedroom and shut the door, leaving her with the pillow clasped against her like a shield, and when she had gone she punched it with clenched fists.

It seemed unwise to sleep in the silk dress and after a few minutes she thought it safe to take it off, wrapping the tartan blanket round her instead. She was about to settle herself on the couch when the loudest clap of thunder yet vibrated the whole flat and she shook with uncontrollable fear. Before the final echo had faded she was tapping on his door, the blanket clutched tight at her neck so that she looked like a waif, and in the seconds until he came she couldn't stop shivering. Fortunately, he was still wearing trousers and shirt.

'Would you mind very much leaving your door open while the storm lasts?' she said, wide eyes looking up at him, begging him to understand. 'I think I'd feel much safer.'

Ryan raised one eyebrow and his gaze travelled slowly over her face and down to the tip of the blanket where her toes were the only other part of her showing. They were close to each other, and an awareness suddenly pulsed between them unlike anything Hanna had ever known. Her toes curled into the carpet and she kept her eyes fixed on the medallion that nestled in the dark hair of his chest because she was afraid to meet his eyes. Then he actually laughed without a hint of derision. With his index finger he touched her chin, tilting her face sideways, and his lips brushed her cheek in the merest whisper of a kiss.

'Funny little thing,' he said softly, and walked away leaving the bedroom door wide open.

The couch was surprisingly comfortable. Hanna

seemed to sink into the cushions and pulled the blanket
snuggly round so that it even covered her ears. All the
same, it was impossible to sleep. The crash of thunder
overhead seemed to have been a parting shot, because
from then on it rumbled away into the distance and
only occasional flashes of lightning lit the room, but
rain pounded the windows in unison with her thudding
heart as she lay thinking about Ryan Donalson. Not
that she felt any danger from him, but she was very
conscious of his nearness and was half afraid to close
her eyes.

What kind of man was he? She put his age at about
thirty-five, which was quite old when she compared it
with her own twenty-one years. At that age he ought to
be happily married, or so Hanna thought, but his flat
was bachelor-orientated and it looked as if he had been
alone for quite some time. She tried to recall pieces she
had read about him, but only details of his career came
to mind, the first documentary he made years ago that
caused such a stir, his rise to fame on the strength of it
and his position now at the top of the television tree.
No mention of the women in his life. If only she had
listened more when Jessica talked about him! He loved
Jessica, of course. If the letter she had read was not
proof enough, she had only to remember his voice when
he said there was no comparison between the two of
them. But there must have been other women. Hanna
smiled in the darkness. For sure she was not the first
girl to spend the night in his flat, but she would take a
bet on it that she was the only one to sleep on the couch,
which gave her a certain distinction. Not that his private
life was any of her business, but it passed the time away
trying to picture what sort of girls attracted him. She
imagined they would have to be dark and beautiful like
Jessica, but for some reason she hoped that was not
altogether true.

She intended waking him as soon as she had straightened the couch in the morning, but when she looked in

there was something defenceless about the way he was lying with one arm flung above his head like a small boy and she felt as if she was intruding. Instead she went to the kitchen, plugged in the electric kettle and hunted round for coffee cups. There was a percolator on a shelf, but she didn't know how to use it.

She was glad to see he had moved when she took coffee into the bedroom and he opened his eyes slowly, trying to recall who she was.

'Hello,' she said, brightly, setting the tray down on a low ebony table. 'I'm Hanna Ballantyne, in case you've forgotten.'

Ryan gave a drowsy smile. 'My ministering angel.' A moment later his mouth curled with distaste as he sipped the coffee. 'What on earth do you call this?'

'Coffee.'

'It tastes like diluted cigar ash!'

'I'm afraid I can only make the instant variety,' she said. 'Take it or leave it.'

His eye was looking better, the swelling almost gone, but the colour could have been daubed on from an artist's palette varying from purple to a dirty yellow. His temper rose with the sun that streamed into the room when she pulled the curtains and her pleasure at the lovely view of the Thames from his window was shortlived.

'What in hell time is it?' he demanded, frowning at the brightness.

'In hell I don't know, but here it's nine-fifteen. I came to tell you I'll be on my way now . . .'

'Nine-fifteen!' he yelled. 'Dammit, girl, I'm always at the studios by nine.'

'Well, you won't be today. And I won't get down to Kernsmere unless I leave now. Goodbye, and thank you for letting me shelter from the storm. It's been nice knowing you, Mr Donalson.'

'Wait, Hanna.' He grasped her arm as she passed the bed on her way from the room. 'Wait out there while I dress. I must talk to you.'

She went to the kitchen. From this window she could only see into a yard below, but it had been washed by the torrential rain and now it glistened, bins and milk bottles winking up at her in the sunlight. A few minutes later he joined her, still knotting his tie. His manner this morning was forbidding and she guessed they were in for another difficult day at the studios.

He said: 'Last night was a bit of disaster. I should have taken you home.'

What did he mean? Was he referring to the handbag incident, the blow to his eye, the storm, or her presence in his flat? Perhaps he was now regretting a wasted opportunity.

'I really was anxious for you to have medical attention,' she said, defending her action in case he still had the ridiculous idea that she had forced herself on him. 'My brother had concussion once and nearly died.'

'I'm a survivor,' he said. 'And I do have a bit of common sense, but thanks anyway. I could have got the car out and taken you back to wherever you live, but I suppose you realise I was being a bit bloody-minded.'

There was no apology, but his tone implied one and she knew she could expect nothing more. Ryan Donalson would never say he was sorry. The fact that he could have driven her home himself had not occurred to her, but she was not going to give him the satisfaction of knowing it, so she merely inclined her head with equally vague acknowledgement.

'We'd best forget the whole thing,' she said. 'Perhaps it would have been better if we'd never met, but I'll try not to cross your path again.'

His lips twitched into a smile and he went to the fridge for some mineral water. He poured himself a glass and pushed the bottle over to her. 'Have some. There's bread and marmalade in the cupboard, but I'm afraid there's no time to cook anything.'

She shook her head. 'No, thanks. Just tell me where

the nearest Underground station is from here and I'll leave you in peace, unless what you wanted to say really *is* important.'

'It is.' The kitchen was cluttered with things and it was impossible to see the top of the dresser for books and papers. Ryan sorted out two files and put them in a document case, snapping it shut hurriedly. Then he turned to her with genuine entreaty. 'Hanna, please come with us on Thursday—for Jessica's sake. I know I messed everything up yesterday, said things I didn't mean, but you know I would never do anything to harm her reputation. Her part of the work was finished, other than any alterations we may need when we get out on location, so there's no question of contract breaking. But I know how she hates strangers dabbling with her scripts, and I *know* she wouldn't mind you working on them if she can't be there herself. She's made you sound like the perfect secretary, so, please, won't you reconsider? I'll take full responsibility.'

Hanna was taken by surprise. This new approach made more sense, but she was still reluctant to listen.

'Why couldn't you have spoken like that before?' she said. 'Think of all the trouble you would have saved.'

'You mean you would have come without argument?'

'I mean you wouldn't have got that black eye.'

He gave a second wry smile, but this one had a sly undercurrent. 'I hope you realise I have to find an excuse for it when I get to the studios.'

She weighed the remark up thoughtfully, aware that antagonism was going to be the basis of any encounter with him, and this morning she was not going to be provoked.

'If you're trying verbal blackmail again I'm wise to you, Mr Donalson. It won't work. Nobody at Beauman Studios knows me anyway, so you're quite at liberty to say exactly how you came by it.'

At that he laughed outright. 'Game and set to Miss Ballantyne! I suppose I've jeopardised my chances once more when you were just on the point of saying yes.'

'Was I?'

'Come now, for a few seconds there I could see the Mississippi River reflected in your eyes.'

The sun lent a golden glow to the kitchen and through the window across the hall she caught a glimpse of two bright little boats chugging up river towards Putney with a distinct holiday air. It was true, in a few days' time she could be looking out at the Mississippi. There really wasn't any valid reason why she shouldn't let a cherished dream come true, not now he had re-phrased the request. Ryan Donalson was a misfortune she would have to put up with, but perhaps he wouldn't need her too much and she would try to keep out of his way. All she had to do was phone Aunt Rachael and a room would be ready for her, so there wouldn't be any meeting up with him once filming was over for the day.

He was waiting for an answer.

'All right,' she said, 'I'll come, as long as you inform Jessica that I didn't skip off to America for the fun of it as soon as her back was turned.'

'I said I would accept responsibility,' he repeated. 'You know, she'll never believe it took so long to persuade you.'

A jet thundered low overhead as it came in to land at Heathrow, and Hanna shivered with a mixture of excitement and apprehension. What was she letting herself in for? She was a secretary, not a writer. She didn't want to let anybody down, especially Jessica, and the enormity of what she was agreeing to was staggering. But Ryan had insisted.

'By the way,' he said, 'take that green dress with you. It suits you.'

The stubborn streak in her made her want to refuse, but it seemed Ryan Donalson had a habit of getting his own way, and she knew the dress would probably find its way into her case.

CHAPTER FOUR

FROM then on everything happened so fast that by the time she arrived in Vicksburg Hanna was remembering the days between as just a succession of fleeting incidents. Luckily she already had a passport and visa. Before getting the job with Jessica she had planned to visit Aunt Rachael and had made sure her papers were ready in good time, but the visit had had to be postponed. It seemed unbelievable that she was now going out there with a television company.

When she got back from Kernsmere it left only one day to sort out any work that needed finishing at the mews house, and to do all her packing. She wrote Jessica a carefully worded note and left it propped against the typewriter, though she hoped to be back herself first so that she could give a proper explanation. There was certainly no time to spare for doubts, even if she had been left with any after her mother's excited reception of the news. The main problem after her visit home was to find room for all the presents her mother had found to send to her sister, and she wondered what comment would be made when she arrived at the airport with an extra suitcase.

It seemed like chaos in the departure lounge at the airport, and she hardly saw Ryan at all. He was busy organising the equipment that had to be taken. But he did find a moment to introduce her to a girl called Vicki Lander who was in charge of costumes.

'Hanna is deputising for Jessica,' he said. 'Look after her, Vicki, there's a good girl. She's not safe to be out alone.'

Vicki looked from one to the other and raised an inquisitive eyebrow as she sensed the antagonism between them.

49

Hanna ignored him and smiled warmly at Vicki. 'Actually I'm quite good at taking care of myself. I'm afraid Mr Donalson has a strange sense of humour.' She held out her hand to the other girl. 'Hello, Vicki, I'm very pleased to meet you.'

'We'd better stick together,' said Vicki. 'Females seem to be in the minority this trip.' Then she turned to Ryan. 'By the way, I saw about Jessica's wedding in the paper this week. Hard luck, Ryan. How come *you* missed the boat?'

There was a definite lowering of the temperature, though only his eyes narrowed to show his displeasure at the intrusion in his personal affairs. Vicki was overstepping the mark and he didn't like it.

'Let's say I prefer not be classed as mediocre,' he said, and left Vicki to puzzle over the answer, because obviously she had not read Alistair's article.

Mediocrity was not a word that could ever be applied to Ryan Donalson. Hanna watched him elbow his way through the crowd, expecting people to move for him, and his air of authority drew attention. This was the man she had tried to fight against only two nights ago, and she realised now how much she had dreaded meeting him this morning. He was too powerful. No one stood a chance against him if he was set on a certain plan, and it was no reflection on her strength of will that she had finally agreed to come on this trip. He had won, but that didn't mean he could say what he liked to her. She was going to make sure her dealings with him over the next few days were strictly businesslike with no more unfortunate clashes like the one she now thought of as the Gambria episode. Every time she recalled it she burned with embarrassment.

A shiver of apprehension stole over her and she found she could not look away from the place across the room where Ryan's curly head was visible above the crowd. The meeting with him today hadn't been too bad after all, but she hoped he would never refer to the bruise on

his face in front of anyone. It was the first thing she had
looked at when he came up to her and she had been
relieved to see the state of his eye vastly improved and
the bruise almost gone, but crude jokes about it would
be very hard to take while she was among so many
strangers.

It had been nice of him to introduce her to Vicki,
and she glanced round, determined not to let Ryan
dominate her thoughts a moment longer. Vicki would
think her a dead loss as a companion if she didn't
make an effort at conversation and she turned to her
with a bright comment ready, only to stop in surprise.
The other girl was staring across the room just as
Hanna had been doing, her eyes fixed on Ryan. Then
she became aware of Hanna's curiosity and gave a
philosophical laugh.

'Oh, well,' she said, 'with Jessica out of the way I
suppose there'll be a chance for someone else.'

'If anyone can stand him,' said Hanna.

She liked Vicki Lander. She was a sophisticated girl in
some ways, but there was a spontaneity about her that
was refreshing and Hanna was glad of her company.
The leading actors kept very much to themselves and
the technicians formed a close group of their own, so
without Vicki to talk to it would have been a long and
lonely journey.

'Did you design all the costumes for *The Forty-seven
Days*?' Hanna asked her when they were airborne and
exploring various topics of conversation.

'Good gracious, no! Wish I had.' Vicki was sketching
dresses round the edge of a magazine page. 'I'd love to
be a designer. All I do is look after the wardrobe and
see everything is pressed, or in the right condition for
whatever scene they're shooting.'

'Some of the dresses are beautiful.'

'Yes,' said Vicki. 'Only the best is good enough for
Ryan's productions.'

Her own clothes were stylish and not quite the sort

that Hanna would have chosen, but their flamboyance typified the kind of person she was and she could get away with it. The white cotton trench-style dress, tightly belted with carmine leather that exactly matched her carmine-coloured lipstick, would probably get dirty long before Hanna's neat grey flannel blazer and skirt, but it was Vicki who would get noticed, and for the first time Hanna wondered if perhaps there was something to be said for clothes that would cost double in cleaning bills. For travelling she had drawn her curly auburn hair into a sensible knot on top of her head, but Vicki's fair hair lay thick across the back of the seat, seemingly tangled waves arranged with costly care to give a provocative effect. She was beautiful. And having seen the expression in her eyes when she looked at Ryan, Hanna wondered how long it would be before she replaced Jessica in his life, because she was hoping to catch him, that was for sure. Hanna silently wished her luck.

'Have you known Ryan long?' asked Vicki, as if tuning in on the same wavelength.

'Since Monday,' said Hanna. 'How about you?'

Vicki stared straight ahead to where Ryan was sitting only a few rows in front of them. 'I was there when he first came to Beauman Studios. Wow! All the girls were after him, especially when they found out he wasn't married. I think he brought Jessica Franklin along as a sort of protection. She soon showed everyone who he belonged to. I gather it was a live-in relationship, which is as good as marriage to my mind. I'd settle for that with a man like Ryan any day.'

'But it didn't last,' Hanna reminded her. She was old-fashioned enough to believe that marriage was important and did not entirely agree with the other girl's views, though it wouldn't do to say so. And she felt strangely indignant that it was assumed Jessica and Ryan were living together at one time. Certainly if there had been that kind of relationship it must have come to an end before she started working at the mews house.

Was that what the letter had been about? Of course, it all fitted into place. Jessica had grown tired of him being there and he had written to her, begging her to reconsider. Probably he had even asked her to marry him and she had refused. An unexpected rush of sympathy welled up in her at the way Jessica had treated him, though no doubt he deserved it if he was as high-handed with her as he was with everyone else. Anyway, Hanna resolved to make a few allowances for him if he proved to be too unbearable.

But her sympathy soon evaporated when a stewardess came along with their lunches. She was a very attractive brunette with a trilby-type hat set forward on upswept hair and glamour surrounded every move she made. When she got to Ryan he gave her a devastating smile and she responded in kind. It sickened Hanna to see the way he then tried to chat her up and she was glad when the girl's cool reaction cancelled out the first smile. It served him right!

Vicki had been to America before, but to Hanna everything was new and exciting. Changing planes at New York, and landing at Allen Thompson Field, the air terminal at Jackson, Mississippi, were all part of the excitement, and though it was like stepping into a hot-house when she left the air-conditioned building the humidity failed to dampen her spirits even for a second. She could see why Vicki had worn a cotton dress. The difference between the crisp, cool early morning air when they left Gatwick and this heavy heat was something no one had described.

It was about an hour's drive from Jackson to Vicksburg and arrangements had been made for them to stay in a hotel overnight and finish the journey the next day, except for Ryan who had a hired car waiting so that he could go on ahead and make sure there would not be any hitches to delay the start of filming.

'We're on a tight budget,' he said, when someone asked if he was not too tired. 'I can't afford to waste time sorting out wrongly allocated rooms or anything like that tomorrow, so I'd rather press on now. And I guarantee I'll be working before any of you in the morning, so don't let me hear any of you complaining of jet lag, because I shan't have any sympathy.'

'Tyrant!' said Bill Hickly, one of the cameramen. 'Never knew such a glutton for work!'

'Pity a few of *you* don't feel the same. It's no good thinking you're here to have a good time, because you're not.'

Harsh words. Hanna looked at the people round her, expecting a cross reaction, but no one took any notice of his lowered brows and stern expression. In fact, Bill Hickly looked quite unconcerned.

'Don't forget, Ryan, it's six o'clock here, but it must be getting on for midnight back home. Don't push yourself too hard.'

'Don't kid yourself,' laughed one of the other men. 'He's after picking himself the best bird in town before we have a chance!'

Ryan smiled and nodded slowly. 'How did you guess?' He pulled at the knot of his tie and opened his shirt at the neck, stretching his chin with relief. 'One thing, there can't be any ice maidens like the one on the plane. They wouldn't last two minutes in this heat!'

Everyone laughed and started joking and Ryan joined in. Hanna stood a little way apart, not knowing them well enough to take part in the play of words, and after a while she went over to a couch and sat down. The hotel lounge was crowded and she hadn't the courage to go and ask the number of her room before everyone else did the same. It was like a dream listening to the American voices around her, and when Ryan called her name in his very precise English, it was like a command.

'Hanna.' He came over to her. 'If you want extra time with your relations I'll take you with me. That's if you're not too tired.'

The condition was thrown in like a challenge and she

straightened her shoulders automatically, raising a barrier of self-defence. If he didn't really want to take her, why had he offered? She was on the point of declining, partly because she really was tired, but mainly because it would mean at least an hour alone in his company and she had resolved to avoid close contact with him. But the thought of getting to Aunt Rachael's earlier was very tempting, and would be better than staying overnight in a strange hotel.

So she said: 'Thank you, I'd like to come. I hope you know the way.'

'Since it's straight through on the Interstate I think I'll manage.' His tone had an edge to it, probably because he was tired, too, though he would never admit it.

'Good,' said Hanna. 'So if you feel like dropping off to sleep it will be easy enough for me to take over the driving.'

The muscles of his face tightened and she was afraid she had gone too far, but he ignored her remark and went back to the men. Why did she keep having to try and get the better of him? It had been kind of him to offer her a lift and she was grateful. She would have to curb this dreadful urge to score off him every time they met if she was going to survive the trip, for after all, he was the most important man around here, the one who called the tune, and it was not very clever to test his patience all the time. For the life of her she couldn't think what made her want to do it. It never happened with anyone else.

She slipped quietly out of the hotel lounge, after a brief word to Vicki, and went to wait in the foyer.

'Get yourselves a good night's sleep,' she heard Ryan say. 'Charge up your drinks to expenses, and I'll expect you in Vicksburg by mid-morning. Everything's arranged.'

He followed her into the foyer, collected the car keys from the desk and picked up his battered leather holdall and one of her cases, motioning to her to bring the other. There was no one to open the door, so he pushed it with one shoulder and waited for her to pass him, not even looking at her.

'You don't really have to see about rooms, do you?' she asked as they got in the car. It seemed too menial a task for a director.

The tension eased and he grinned like a schoolboy caught out making false excuses. 'I needed to get away from the crowd. I guess I'm not very sociable after a long journey.'

'So why did you ask me to come along if you wanted to be alone?'

'I didn't say I wanted to be alone.' He started the engine and drove out of the hotel forecourt with the confidence of someone well used to handling large American cars. 'I took pity on you. You were looking a bit lost among so many strangers.'

'I didn't mind,' she said. Then, not wanting to sound ungrateful, she added: 'But I'd much rather get to Vicksburg. I can't wait to meet my aunt and cousins.'

'You ought to have phoned them from the hotel.'

'Never mind, I'll do it when we get there. They'll be surprised to hear me a day early.' She snuggled into the wide, well-upholstered seat with a little sigh and looked around her. 'It's a fantastic car. What make is it?'

'A Buick Le Sabre.'

'I've never been in one so grand.'

'The hire firm called it a loaded car,' he said, 'meaning everything is automatic. There's also a CB radio so that I can call for help if you attack me again.'

She laughed. 'You're not afraid of me, surely?'

'You'd be surprised,' he said. There was a hint of humour in the words, but something in his tone suggested a deeper meaning which puzzled her.

She glanced at him sharply, not trusting him to leave it there, but he was concentrating on the road and made no further comment. A silence lengthened between them and she turned half sideways in her seat so that she

could observe him unobtrusively, wondering what
thoughts went on in that handsome head. Was he
wishing it was Jessica there beside him? His hands rested
lightly on the wheel, long, powerful hands that could
grip like a vice. She drew a quick breath, recalling the
strength of his arms that night in his flat, and not even
the air-conditioning could cool the warmth of her face
as she remembered the bruising, unnecessary kiss he had
given her. She looked at his mouth and her own lips
tingled. Indignation still burned in her, yet a strange
pulsing through her body as she studied him gave the lie
to it. There was no denying his male magnetism, only
where she was concerned it was a case of repel rather
than attract. In the closeness of the car she had to try to
be pleasant, but nothing changed the hostility she felt.

There was so much to see driving out of Jackson along
the freeway. She turned from Ryan and looked out of
the window, not wanting to miss anything. Signs in
colourful confusion lined the roadside, illuminated as
evening drew on, and so many of them advertised food
and eating places she wondered whether Americans did
anything else but eat and drink. It was a whole new
world. And the size of the cars everywhere made her
feel as if she was watching a movie. But once they had
left the town behind them there was nothing but acres
of fields not long planted, and the long, straight road
swept past them like a thread of grey ribbon that had
no end.

'That's cotton,' said Ryan, breaking the silence and
answering her unspoken question.

'You mean growing in those fields?' She sat up to
look more carefully, though there was hardly anything
to see.

'That's right. Pity it isn't cotton picking time.'

'Oh, yes,' she said, 'I'd love to be here then.' It
conjured up a colourful picture of riverboats, cotton
bales and women in gingham dresses singing the old
songs in rich, Southern voices. She sighed and smiled to

herself, knowing how silly he would think her if he knew.
That was what came of watching romantic old films like
Showboat, and she began singing softly, 'Tote that
barge, lift that bale.' To her amazement Ryan joined in,
a good tenor voice giving weight to the words, and they
finished in unison, laughing together at the end of it.

Then a thought occurred to her that brought a frown,
and she looked at him suspiciously.

'How did you know it was cotton?' she asked.

He stretched back in the seat, easing his arms. 'It
looks the same as it did last time I was here.'

'Last time?' Hanna exclaimed. 'You led me to believe
you'd never been to Vicksburg before.'

'I didn't say that.'

'But you asked me all those questions, as if you
wanted to know what it was like.' To be so deliberately
misleading was paramount to lying in Hanna's estima-
tion, and she was bristling with resentment.

'I asked because I wanted to know whether you were
really involved with Jessica's work, or merely a typist. If
you were involved you would want to make sure all
went well on location and I could trust you.'

It made sense, but it did not alter the fact that he had
not been completely honest with her, and while he now
apparently felt he could rest assured the scripts were in
reasonably good hands, he had done nothing to improve
Hanna's opinion of him. He was a ruthless, scheming
rogue and she wished she had not walked into his trap
so blindly.

'It wasn't necessary to treat me like a child, letting me
ramble on ad nauseam about my relatives because I
thought you were interested,' she said.

'I was, and *am*, interested. I'm sorry if you're
offended. Your young cousins sound like a lot of fun
and I'm looking forward to meeting them. I like Americans.'

It was hard to tell whether he was being serious or
patronising. If only they were in sight of Vicksburg so

that she could soon get away from him! Her hands were clasped tightly in her lap to stop her fidgeting with her skirt. He unnerved her, made her feel awkward.

'Jessica told me about the time she came here,' she went on. 'She said if only she'd thought of *The Forty-seven Days* then she would have been able to collect so much more material, but she didn't start writing it for quite a while. That's why she was pleased about my aunt. Having a contact in Vicksburg made it easier to get information.' She paused. Then: 'She didn't ever say that you knew it, too.' It was ridiculous to be resentful, but she couldn't help it. If he had levelled with her from the beginning it would have simplified matters and they could have talked without restraint.

Ryan said nothing for a few minutes and his eyes scanned the horizon with equal hope that the road didn't really go on for ever. Then those eyes were on Hanna, observing her inscrutably.

'As a matter of fact,' he said, 'Jessica and I were here together. She probably didn't tell you that. But as you're so keen to learn everything about me you may as well know I first met Jessica at a jazz festival in New Orleans a couple of years ago. We liked the country so much we stayed on and toured up through Mississippi. You could say those were the good days.'

He was quietly putting her in her place and she felt duly chastised.

'I'm sorry . . .'

'There's no need to be.'

'But I didn't know you had personal memories of this place. It must be a bit of an ordeal for you to come back right now. If only you'd explained . . .'

'There was nothing to explain,' said Ryan. 'And just for the record, *The Forty-seven Days* was my idea, not Jessica's. I was the one who persuaded her to write it.'

'You?'

'Yes.' He smiled dryly at her surprise. 'There's something about Vicksburg that got under my skin. I couldn't get it out of my mind. You'll see for yourself, and if you're the girl I think you are I wouldn't mind betting it'll have the same effect on you.' They were coming into the town at last and he indicated parkland lying over to the right. A monument was just discernible in the half light, a suggestion of hills, a large modern building close to the road. 'That's the National Military Park—sixteen miles of it. I guarantee you'll come away from there a different person from when you went in. I never realised the Civil War was such a terrible thing until I saw how close the trenches were, and how many died in the most appalling conditions. It brought a pain to my guts, and that's the plain truth. I wanted to show what it was like for the people of Vicksburg, cooped up here for all those days with food running short and bombardments and fighting all around them.'

'It's happened in other places,' she reminded him. 'In the first world war, the Napoleonic wars . . .'

'Yes, but not brother fighting against brother. Some of those men knew each other. They didn't want to fight, but they had to because they happened to have been born north or south of a line, and a good percentage of them were hardly more than children. Did you know that at night when the firing stopped they used to meet on ground between the lines and chat?'

'I read all the books Jessica had,' said Hanna. 'I used to take them home with me.'

'But until you've seen where it happened you can't begin to understand the tragedy of it.'

He went on discussing it with her as they drove into town, giving an insight to the depth of his feelings for this incident in history, and because Hanna had become totally absorbed in it while typing the script she lost her reticence and shared his view knowledgeably. For the first time in their short acquaintance she found something exhilarating in his company, and when he finally turned a corner and swung into a car park behind a big motel her relief was tinged with regret. Jessica had made a wonderful job of the script, but she had never enjoyed the research as Hanna had done. There had been no one to share her keen interest. But Ryan Donalson was steeped in Civil War history and it was such a pity there was not going to be any more time to talk about it.

'This is it,' he said, pulling into a convenient parking space. 'Headquarters for the next couple of weeks.'

He got out of the car, slamming the door behind him, and went round to the boot to unload their luggage. Hanna wrestled with the door handle her side, but for some reason it refused to move. She pushed it, pulled it, pressed it, but still nothing happened.

'We're here,' Ryan said impatiently, tapping on the glass as if she intended staying there all night.

She wound the window down. 'I can't get out.'

She tried the handle again and leaned her weight against the door just as Ryan touched it from the outside, and the next thing she knew she was tumbling out and would have landed on the ground if he hadn't been there to catch her. He lifted her up and for a moment she was held against him so that she could feel the heat of his body through the fine cotton shirt.

She drew away from him quickly. Her head was spinning. Just for a second her hand had rested on his warm brown arm and the hair beneath her fingers was like a hundred small shocks that disturbed her heart rate. When she looked up at him the familiar frown creased his brows. The expression in his eyes was unfathomable. She thought he was angry with her for being clumsy, but he made no comment at all, and when she steadied herself against the bonnet of the car he made no further move. It was ridiculous to recoil from him like that, but physical contact had set her quivering as if she had touched a live wire and reaction made her legs tremble. Perhaps it was the heat. Even now the sun had gone the temperature felt as if it was still in the eighties. Her skin was damp and her skirt clung uncomfortably to her tights.

She gave a shaky laugh. 'Well, if this is a fully automatic car give me my little old jalopy at home any day! At least I never get locked in.'

'A little patience and little less panic would have helped,' he said.

'You could have had the manners to open the door for me in the first place,' she retorted.

He raised one eyebrow. 'Thank God we weren't *both* locked in.'

Strength returned to her legs, and she grabbed hold of both her cases before he could offer to carry one, marching ahead of him in the direction of the motel entrance.

'If you care to show me where there's a phone I'll get through to my aunt straight away. You won't need to put up with me for much longer.'

'Perhaps I ought to warn your relations what they're letting themselves in for.'

He was behind her and she couldn't see his face, but though the tone of his voice had hardly altered she knew he was laughing. Damn the man! He was more irritating by the hour.

The phone went on ringing and ringing. Hanna listened to the unfamiliar tone with growing concern and finally put the receiver down.

'There's no answer. They must be out.'

Ryan sauntered over. 'Must be making the most of their last free evening before you arrive,' he teased, then sensed her anxiety and his voice softened. 'You look tired, Hanna. Are you all right?'

'Yes, I'm fine,' she said. She was a bit lightheaded and her legs felt weak, as though she might keel over at any minute, but as the reason for it dawned on her her lips twitched into a smile. 'To be honest I'm absolutely starving!'

He was instantly contrite. 'I'm sorry, I should have thought of food earlier. We haven't eaten since we were on the plane. Tell you what, there's a very good restaurant here, so if we check in and have a quick shower we should then be able to do justice to a meal. What do you think?'

'I'll wait for you here.' The thought of a shower was bliss, but she was not staying at the motel.

'Of course, you were going to Aunt Rachael's,' he said, slapping the palm of his hand against his forehead. He glanced at his watch. 'Seems to me you've got two choices. Either you can use my shower, or you can assume your family won't be back till late as they weren't expecting you, and stay on here for the night.'

The thought of using the shower in his room when there was every chance he might not do the gentlemanly thing and stay out of the way made her hotter than ever, and tiredness was playing funny tricks. Much as she disliked being with Ryan, even his company this evening now seemed preferable to meeting strangers and having to make excited conversation. She would make a much better impression if she waited until morning when she would be refreshed from a good night's sleep.

'I think I'd like to stay on here,' she said, 'if that's all right.'

'Sensible girl.' He took a look at the sky through the window and turned back to her philosophically. 'Reckon it'll be safe enough to book us two single rooms. It doesn't look as if there's going to be a storm tonight.'

He was teasing again, surely? He couldn't possibly be sounding her out to see what his chances were. Or could he?

'There'll be a storm all right if I find you've made any other arrangements,' she said primly.

He gave a wicked smile, and went off to book two rooms.

That night Hanna just couldn't get to sleep. Vicksburg traffic was not too noisy, but she was conscious of it, and her mind was too active for her to relax. Earlier she had changed into a lavender blue dress with soft pleats and no sleeves to go down to the Plantation Restaurant, and Ryan had given her an approving nod even though he passed no comment. And the meal had been out of this world—chicken and pineapple salad served up on half of the largest fresh pineapple she had ever seen, with so many other delicacies added she lost count, and her first taste of real Bourbon pie to follow. The only mistake she made was asking for a Martini to drink. It turned out to be largely gin and it was a job to keep her eyes open and her mind alert enough to cope with conversation. It was surprising, then, that she was unable to sleep.

After a while she got up and made herself coffee from the machine by her sink unit, and with the cup between her hands she stood in the middle of the room and went over the events of the last few hours until she came to the few minutes before she had said goodnight to Ryan outside her door. It was not that he had appeared to expect anything of her. On the contrary, hc kept his hands against his sides and carefully avoided the slightest touch, but his eyes looked into hers in such a way that her temples started to throb. It must have been the Martini that affected her vision. She could have sworn there was a kind of yearning in that penetrating gaze, and the strange thing was it didn't frighten her. But it did disturb her, because through the haze of tiredness he awakened a new kind of restlessness in herself which she didn't want to analyse. She wanted to keep him there longer so that she wouldn't have to go into an empty room where she would be quite alone in a new country. Yet if he had made one move to enter the room with her she would have been furiously angry.

After what seemed an eternity he broke the spell with a jerk of his head.

'Goodnight,' he said. 'Sleep well.' And he strode off along the balcony which linked all the rooms on that floor, letting himself into one two doors away.

Perhaps he did not want to be alone either, here in the very town where he had been so happy with Jessica.

This location trip couldn't have come at a worse time for him. The irony of it struck her forcibly. Who knew, perhaps he had been making plans to revive the love affair that surely should have led to marriage, and it must be heartbreaking for him to think of her now married to someone else. No wonder he had wanted to come on ahead of the others! In the few hours' breathing space before they joined him he would be able to re-adjust to being in Vicksburg without Jessica. Of course, the searching look she had seen in his eyes was simply regret that he was standing there with the wrong girl. How different things might have been for him.

Anyway, why was she wasting time thinking of Ryan Donalson when there was so much else going on in her own life? There was a whole new world out there beckoning and she was longing for the morning. She felt as if Vicksburg was slumbering under a warm cover, and tomorrow she would flick the cover off and see all the interesting places that had been just tantalising sil-houettes in the dusk as they drove in. Why, it might even be possible to see the Mississippi from her window, and that was the most delicious thought. She was look-ing forward to seeing that mighty river almost as much as seeing Aunt Rachael and the boys for the first time.

She finished her coffee and decided to take one more little peep at Vicksburg before going back to bed, and as she opened the door quietly she felt like a child undoing a birthday parcel that was meant to be hidden until the morning. A rush of warm air greeted her, and she was just about to step out into the open when she realised someone else was there. Ryan was leaning over the balustrade outside his room. It was not easy to move back inside without him hearing and she stayed in the shadows for several minutes with her arms clasped tight across her flimsy cotton nightie. He wore only his trousers. In the moonlight his broad shoulders gleamed and the lines of his face in profile were etched against the silver night sky.

Hanna was acutely aware of him. Every nerve in her body tingled and she found she was holding her breath so long there was a pain in her chest. What was it about him that filled her with such disquiet? The cold surface of the balcony began to chill her feet and a shiver went through her in spite of the warm air, but she didn't move. She couldn't take her eyes off him. Then, as if the intensity of her thoughts communicated itself to him, he gradually turned his head, and the awareness became mutual.

She heard his low, seductive voice say just one word.

'Hanna?' It was a question very softly spoken.

Like a dancer she trembled on tiptoe for an indecisive second, then fled back to her room and turned the key.

CHAPTER FIVE

'HANNA!' Aunt Rachael gave a shriek of delight at the sound of her niece's voice when she telephoned first thing in the morning. 'Oh, honey, it's so good to hear you. When did you get in? Where are you now?'

A string of questions followed without a break and Hanna was laughing on the phone at such a joyous welcome. It was some time before she could find space to answer.

'I'm at the motel where the television crew will be staying. I phoned you last night . . .'

'Last night? Oh, Hanna, we had to go to a charity gala at Leigh's college. If only I'd known!'

'It doesn't matter. You're there now and I can't wait to see you.'

'Honey, we'll be over just as soon as we can make it. Jay, Hanna's here!' Aunt Rachael yelled to her son with growing excitement, then spoke to Hanna again. 'I'll have that boy out of the bath and into the car before he's had a chance to dry off. We'll be with you in about an hour and a half.'

Hanna put the phone down thoughtfully. The sun was out, it was a glorious day, and she was so impatient to meet her relations she had been prepared to forgo breakfast, but they wouldn't be here for some time yet. She would have to wait a little longer.

There had been no sign of Ryan when she came downstairs. Evidently he was sleeping off his nocturnal vigil. As she was going to have to have breakfast after all she decided not to wait for him. It would taste better without distraction, and she was not anxious to face him across the table at such an early hour.

She was on her second cup of coffee when he finally

appeared. He wore a blue gingham shirt open almost to
the waist, and denim jeans that fitted tight across his
hips and thighs, casual clothes which made him look
quite different, and admiring glances from the waitresses
followed him as he walked over to Hanna's table with a
lithe grace. It was fascinating the way women responded
to him.

She had been wrong about him sleeping late. His hair
was wet, matted curls glistening, and a smell of fresh
morning air clung to him as he came up to her and
touched her shoulder. She jerked her spine ramrod-
straight. His hand was cool through the cheesecloth
blouse she was wearing and she wanted to shrug him off.

'You should have come for a swim, Hanna,' he said.
'I had the pool to myself.'

'I didn't think you would be up so early.'

'I've been working since six. I don't need much sleep.'
He sat down opposite her and ordered breakfast, smiling
up at the waitress with a devastating charm that
sickened Hanna. She was sorry the girl didn't give him
a cool brush-off, but there was no hope of that. Ryan's
swim had revived his spirits miraculously and he was so
full of good humour she hardly recognised him. When
she was also treated to one of his smiles she was glad he
had bestowed the first one on the waitress, otherwise
she would have been tempted to think it was meant ex-
clusively for her. He said: 'You looked pensive when I
came in. What was on your mind?'

She wanted to say, 'Not you,' because in his arrogance
he no doubt hoped anything that disturbed her was at-
tributable to him, but she held her tongue. Instead she
kept on a safe subject.

'I phoned my aunt before breakfast. She said she'd be
over in about an hour and a half. I thought she would
come straight round.'

'Perhaps she had a few jobs to see to first. Whereabouts in Vicksburg does she live?'

'Port Gibson, just down the road.'

At that Ryan threw back his head and laughed. 'My dear girl, you haven't taken into the account the little matter of American exaggeration. When they say just down the road it can mean anything. Port Gibson happens to be about thirty miles away.'

She stared at him in disbelief. 'You can't mean it!'

'I certainly mean it. And I hope you realise you've got to report in for work every morning from there. We make an early start, you know, before all the sightseers get about.'

He buttered a roll, giving it all his attention while she adjusted to the idea.

'I thought I'd be able to walk to work, or get a bus,' she said, almost to herself. 'What am I going to do?'

'Don't worry,' he consoled her, 'people out here are used to driving long distances. All you have to do is make sure you go to bed early so that you can get up in good time.' He paused, letting his eyes rest on her a moment contemplatively. Then: 'Oh, and a word of advice, Hanna. Don't pad around at night in your nightie. Someone might get the wrong idea.'

Her face flamed. How dared he talk as if she had opened her door last night to deliberately encourage him! It was the last thing she would ever want to do ... the very last thing. If he had had any sense of discretion he wouldn't even have mentioned the incident.

'I do *not* pad around in my nightie, as you put it,' she retorted, seething.

'Pity,' said Ryan. 'You made a very pretty picture.'

She stood up quickly, pushing back her chair with such force it nearly tipped over. 'Mr Donalson, I shall go and wait for my aunt somewhere else. If you want to discuss work with me I shall be in the lounge. Otherwise I don't think we have anything to talk about.'

She reached for her bag, a small cream canvas one that matched her sandals, but before she could pick it up he grasped her hand.

'The name is Ryan,' he said. 'Try it, Hanna—it won't

hurt, I promise. If you go calling me Mr Donalson in front of the crew they'll wonder who the hell you're on about.'

She kept her lips firmly closed, defying him silently, and after a minute he let her hand go. My round, she thought, but for some reason there was not the same satisfaction in it as there had been a few days ago. The pressure of his fingers left a burning sensation, as if he had marked her, and to her increasing annoyance she saw he was laughing at her.

'Smile,' he coaxed. 'I know you disapprove of me, but maybe if you could stop showing it for a while we might be able to put up with each other better. You've got a very nice nose.'

Her hand went up automatically to touch her nose and as she kept it there the corners of her mouth began to turn up until she was laughing with him.

'That's twice you've tried to flatter me today,' she said, sitting down again in the chair. 'I'm getting suspicious, Ryan Donalson. What do you want me to do?'

'There, you said it!' He slapped the table loudly, making people look round.

'Said what?'

'My name. You see, it was easy, wasn't it? Now say it again.'

'Ryan,' she said primly.

He sighed, not completely satisfied. 'Well, I suppose that'll have to do. Looks like it's going to be a slow thaw.'

There was no accounting for this new, frivolous mood and she tried not to respond to it too readily. The sun was on him, lending a glow to his skin, but it also showed up the bruise on his temple which had faded to almost nothing in ordinary light, and she was reminded of their previous encounter. Take care, she warned herself. But when his eyes were on her with that mock severity she could see why other women found him so attractive, and pressed her lips even tighter together because she had lost the round to him after all.

'Better let me tell you what the plans are for filming,' he said, breaking a brief silence filled with undercurrents. He clasped his hands behind his neck and got down to business. 'Today I'm going to drive round the location sites with Bill Hickly and see what sets the unit manager has arranged for tomorrow. Probably outside the Old Court House might be best as it's the weekend. There won't be so much traffic to be diverted. I have to get on to the authorities. Then I want to get shots of the Balfour House in the can as soon as possible.'

'That's one place I really want to see,' said Hanna. 'I've read quite a bit about Emma Balfour.'

The first episode of *The Forty-seven Days* was all about the start of the Vicksburg Siege and events immediately prior to it. In a way it was Hanna's favourite episode because it was full of elegance and grandeur, the gracious way of Southern living before war came to the town and changed everything, and the beauty of it contrasted vividly with the ravages that followed. A wonderful Christmas Eve Ball was in full swing in the home of Dr and Mrs Balfour in the year 1862. They were entertaining Confederate officers and their ladies, and among the many distinguished guests were General Lee and General Martin Luther Smith. Emma Balfour, the doctor's wife, was a perfect hostess and the Ball was the most talked about event of the Christmas season, but at the height of the festivities a messenger burst in with news that Union gunboats with Federal troops aboard were approaching Vicksburg. The Yankees were coming. It was the start of the Siege. The gaiety came abruptly to an end and General Smith began mobilising the Rebel troops right there in the house. Most of the episode, of course, had already been filmed with interior sets in the studio back home, but there were scenes which needed original backgrounds and the beautiful antebellum houses, the Balfour house among them, could never be reconstructed with anything like authenticity.

Ryan began to tell Hanna how he intended using the outdoor shots and she listened attentively. He had clever ideas which required a minimum cast with maximum effect, and as he described different aspects she found her admiration for his work growing. No matter what she might think of him personally there was no denying his brilliance as a director.

So engrossed did she become in the techniques of television production, it was something of an intrusion when a waitress came up and asked if she was Miss Hanna Ballantyne from England. Hanna looked up in surprise.

'Yes,' she said, 'I'm Hanna Ballantyne.' Whereupon the waitress stepped back and in her place was an incredibly good-looking young man, at least six feet tall, with the shoulders of a baseball player and thick fair hair that sat across his forehead like a thatch. He wore a green T-shirt with the name of his college written across the front, and white jeans, the brightness of which were matched only by the sparkle of his teeth when he smiled to greet her after staring spellbound for several seconds.

'Why, cousin Hanna,' he said, 'I sure am going to enjoy escorting you round this little ole town. I'm Jay Caldwell.'

She couldn't believe her eyes. Was this the cousin she had thought of as a boy? He was a young giant, and when he held out his arms she went straight into them and hugged him as if she had known him for years.

'Jay, I'm *so* pleased to see you!' It was some time before she could extricate herself from his rapturous embrace, and she began to feel embarrassed, conscious of Ryan's watchful gaze behind her. Then she looked round eagerly for her aunt, but there was no sign of her. 'Where's your mother?'

'Outside in the car waiting,' said Jay.

'Outside? Why didn't she come in with you?'

He took a deep breath. 'I guess she didn't tell you she doesn't walk too well. Most times she won't even admit it to herself. She hates to be beaten.'

'No,' said Hanna, her face dropping, 'nobody told me. What's the matter with her?'

'Arthritis, but she never complains. Come on, grab your things, she's dying to meet you.'

'And I can't wait to see her. It's what I've come all this way for.'

She was ready to dash off with him, anticipation putting a lilt in her voice, liveliness in every move she made, and Jay was excited, talking quickly about plans he had been making. Ryan coughed pointedly and stood up.

'Hanna has also come out here to work,' he said. 'And as she hasn't the manners to introduce me I'll do it myself. I'm Ryan Donalson, Hanna's boss.'

His tone was coldly polite, but he held out his hand.

'Gee, I'm sorry,' Jay apologised, shaking the proffered hand without much enthusiasm. 'Do I take it you're allowing her time off to get acquainted with her relations?'

The two men were about the same height, but there all similarity ended. An electric fan whirred above their heads, encircling them in a current of air, but the coolness between them was not artificially induced. Hanna looked from one to the other with a frown, perturbed because she had the impression they disliked each other on sight. Not that she could blame Jay. Her own first impression of Ryan had been exactly the same.

'Mr Donalson is *not* my boss,' she said.

'I forgot,' said Ryan to Jay, 'she came with me out of the kindness of her heart.'

She rounded on him immediately, temper rising. 'If you would like me to pay my own expenses I can do so quite easily.'

'I don't understand.' Her cousin blinked, unable to decide whether they shared a private joke, or enjoyed feuding. He'd heard the English humour took some getting used to. 'I thought you were over here with a television company and staying with us meanwhile.'

Hanna started to answer, but Ryan interrupted. 'She can spend the day with you, of course, but take care of her. I'll need her at the Old Court House by eight o'clock tomorrow. Until then you can borrow her.'

What was the matter with him? There was no need for that infuriating superior attitude. The smile had gone from Jay's eyes and Ryan was facing him as though they were about to become sparring partners.

'Please don't talk about me as if I'm some sort of article you're lending out,' she snapped. 'I may be working for you temporarily, but that doesn't give you the right to dictate. Now, if you're sure you can spare me today, we'll be going.' It wasn't like her to be sarcastic, but he asked for it.

'Don't worry, I'll see she's on time in the morning,' said Jay.

'Thank you.' Ryan's lips moved slowly into a half smile, and without warning he bent his head and dropped a kiss on Hanna's cheek. 'Have a good day,' he said, and strode off towards the reception lounge.

Jay stared after him, bemused. 'Is he always like that?'

'He's insufferable,' said Hanna. Her hand had flown to the place where Ryan's mouth had touched. For some reason he had been deliberately putting on an act to impress Jay, and it had been neither clever nor polite to make out he had proprietorial claim on her. As for the parting kiss, it was more like an insult, and she hoped Jay hadn't got the idea she was on too familiar terms with Ryan. 'If it hadn't been for Jessica I would never have come.'

She told him the whole tale of how she came to be involved with the television company as they left the restaurant. It was a relief to be free of Ryan and his complexities for a while and she danced along beside her cousin, the holiday mood catching up with her at last. It was difficult to keep up with his long strides and she was breathless when they reached the car park, but it was only partly due to hurrying. The day had already become full of new experiences.

Aunt Rachael was waiting beside a green convertible and when she saw Hanna she held out her arms the way Jay had done. She was so much like a slightly younger edition of her mother that Hanna laughed with delight as she was enveloped in another bear-hug.

'Oh, Aunt Rachael, this is wonderful!' she breathed.

'Honey, I'm just so thrilled I don't know what to say.' Her aunt was near to tears with happiness.

She was smaller than her mother, but the smile that lit her face was much the same, and her hair was the colour of Hanna's, with hardly a hint of grey in the beautifully styled reddish-brown waves. Her dress was sleeveless cream linen that showed her smooth brown arms to advantage and the straight cut of the skirt disguised a tendency to plumpness that had been noticeable in photographs. Beside this huge son of hers who now hovered protectively she was quite diminutive, and younger-looking than Hanna had pictured her. Certainly she was much too young to be troubled by arthritis. She was a lovely person, and affection welled up in Hanna so that she gave her an extra squeeze before they released each other.

'I'm glad you're like your mother, Hanna,' she said. 'You can tell me all the news from England while we do a bit of sightseeing. Jay, help me in, son. My legs get a bit stiff this time of year—it's so humid. Then later we'll go home and rest while it's hot, and go out for a meal afterwards. Honey, where's your luggage?'

She babbled on while Jay held her arm and eased her into the back of the car.

'I forgot, my two cases are in the foyer,' Hanna laughed. 'I'll get them.'

'Jay'll go, won't you, son? You get in front so you can see everything.'

Hanna slid into the seat as she was told, the leather burning her legs through her thin cheesecloth skirt. She had seen the matching primrose yellow skirt and blouse in a little shop in Kernsmere and was enchanted with the white embroidery on such fine material. It had seemed exactly the thing for a hot climate and her mother had bought it for her as a present. It suited her, she knew, and as she watched Jay go back for her cases she was glad she was looking her best.

Aunt Rachael was still talking, asking questions but not waiting for answers, her lively semi-American accent fascinating to Hanna's ears. She listened, nodded, tried to get a word in, but all she could do was sit back and wait.

'When I had that phone call from your Momma saying you were coming I nearly sat on the cat. We've got a Siamese called Blue and he was right there on the chair. Anyway, I phoned and cancelled two Bridge evenings next week. Do you play Bridge, Hanna? No, I guess you're too young and too busy yet. Leigh isn't so good at sport as Jay. He reads a lot. You'll like him . . .'

It was so hot. Hanna lifted the back of her hair and wished she had knotted it on top the way it had been yesterday. There were no windows open and when she went to open one her aunt stopped her. 'Hey, no, honey! You'll let all the cool air out once we get going and the air-conditioning's on.'

And then she noticed that the car next to them was the one she and Ryan had travelled in the night before. The door was firmly shut, but like a slow action replay she saw herself falling against him when it had burst open, and there was a drumming in her ears that blocked out her aunt's voice. She shut her eyes. No sense thinking about the wretched man and making her temperature rise even further. If only it wasn't so hot.

Jay stowed the cases in the boot and got in the car, switched on and the air began to get cooler.

'Right, cousin Hanna, what would you like to see first?' he asked.

'The river,' she said, clapping her hands, 'I want to see the Mississippi more than anything else.'

They laughed at her eagerness, teased her about it being only an old muddy strip of water, but to Hanna it had always sounded the most romantic river in the world and they were not going to persuade her otherwise.

'Best go up to Fort Hill, Jay,' said Aunt Rachael. 'It looks better from there than down by the levee.'

'That means the National Military Park first, then. Sure you won't be bored, Hanna?'

'Of course I won't be bored. I want to see that, too. And the antebellum houses.'

Aunt Rachael went on talking, explaining about the antebellum houses being mansions built before the Civil War, as if Hanna knew nothing about them, and Jay manoeuvred the car out of the park which was more crowded than it had been the night before.

They were passing the motel entrance when she saw Ryan emerge. His hands were in his pockets and he squinted up at the sun as he came out into the heat. He would be waiting for the crew to arrive. Whereabouts in the city would he go first? In another second they turned the corner and he was lost to view, but she kept looking back and an inexplicable ache started up in her. The breakfast had been richer than anything she was used to, waffles with cream and maple syrup, and she blamed that.

As they drove up through steep brick-lined streets, Jay pointed out places he thought would interest her, and Aunt Rachael kept up a continual commentary on just about everything. The strange ache persisted, like a kind of homesickness which she couldn't account for when she was with relatives who were overwhelmingly pleased to see her. Not until they were actually in the Military Park did it begin to ease. The effect Ryan had said this place would have on her began almost at once.

The sun was beating down from a clear blue sky and green hills shimmered in the heat. It was a beautiful, peaceful place. Who could believe this was once a terrible battlefield, where thousands of lives were lost? There were memorials and statues at every turn commemorating the men who had fought and died, from the ordinary soldier to great leaders on both sides, and when Jay stopped the car at one point to show her a magnificent memorial that looked like the Pantheon in Rome she was dazzled by the sunlight on white stone.

'Let's go and climb up there,' Jay suggested. 'You don't mind, do you, Momma?'

'Of course not. I want you young people to enjoy yourselves.' Aunt Rachael positively beamed.

It took Hanna's breath away. There were so many steps and she was not used to being so hot. Jay waited for her.

'This is a State Memorial,' he said. 'The Illinois one. Each state that took part in the war has one, but this is my favourite.'

'It's certainly impressive,' Hanna agreed.

Inside there were names of men who had fought with Illinois regiments listed all round the single circular room, and the top of the dome was open to the sky.

'They say one of those men was really a woman, but no one found out till years afterwards. Now there's a story for your television company.' He went round the plaques until he came to names beginning with C. 'That's the one, I think, Albert Cashire.'

'I'll tell Jessica,' she said. 'She's always wanting ideas for stories.'

The name was low down and he traced it with his finger. 'He, or she as the case may be, didn't die until about 1911.' He grinned at Hanna and straightened up. 'Shall I tell you another story? There was a veterans' reunion here in 1917, and they were all getting on a bit by then. Do you know, it ended up in fisticuffs and battles with walking sticks and they were all sent home!'

He elaborated on it some more, gesticulating with his

hands, and the picture he created made Hanna hoot with laughter. 'Now that I *must* tell Jessica!'

'You like her a lot, don't you, this Jessica?'

'She's the best possible person to work for.'

He looked at her keenly. 'But you don't go much on that guy Donalson.'

It was not really a question and she let it pass without an answer. A shiver stole over her and she went outside followed by Jay, and at the top of the steps she paused to look across the park. There were a great many markers to show where battalions had fought, so close they seemed only a stone's throw from each other, and Hanna closed her eyes, absorbing the atmosphere.

'How terrible it must have been for all those men,' she said. 'The heat alone would have killed me. How did they stand it out there in trenches in the boiling sun with thick uniforms on?' She pictured scenes from *Gone With The Wind* that she had seen recently at a cinema back home and found it hard to realise that this was the place where truth took over from fiction.

Jay said: 'Yeah, I guess they had a pretty rough time.' But his voice was light and by the direction of his gaze it was obvious he had more pleasant things on his mind. She felt his eyes on her, felt rather than saw the approval in his smile. She was making a hit with her cousin Jay. 'Come on,' he said, 'we've better things to do than look at depressing old battlefields all day.'

He ran down the steps, leaving her to come behind him at a safer pace, and when she reached the bottom he was holding the car door open for her. 'Your car awaits you, ma'am,' he said, with a mock bow.

Aunt Rachael didn't get out of the car at Fort Hill either. Jay led Hanna up a slope, telling her to close her eyes when they were almost at the top. Then he took her hand and guided her to the path at the edge of the bluff.

'Now you can look.'

She opened her eyes, and there was the river, the

Mighty Mississippi, winding its way through green, tree-covered land as far as the eye could see. It was a magnificent view.

'That's Louisiana on the other side,' he said.

'I can't believe I'm really here,' she breathed.

Jay gave her a playful pinch on the arm. 'You're here, Hanna Ballantyne, and I'm real glad you've come. I'm going to take you on the river in the moonlight one evening next week when the moon's full up, so consider yourself dated.'

'Sounds wonderful!'

'With you it will be. I want to show you off to all the guys I know, but I'm scared I might lose you. They're going to just love you.'

He was like an enthusiastic puppy and she played along with him, not taking anything he said seriously. 'Don't worry, Jay, I'll fight them off somehow. I'll tell them all you have prior claim.'

'Do you mean that?' His face lit up. 'I'll hold you to it. You really are the prettiest thing, and ma'am, that's a mighty fine accent you got there. I just love it!'

It was lovely being with someone who could make her laugh so much, and she felt completely at ease with him. Quite casually he slung an arm round her shoulder and pointed to the water below.

'That's the Yazoo River Canal nearest to us. There was a terrific flood not long after the war and the Mississippi changed its course. This hill was one of the Confederate gun emplacements. It commanded the river and they fired on Union gunboats. I think it was this gun that sunk the *Cincinnati*.'

There was a cannon close to where they were standing, its iron barrel pointing across the water, huge wheels rutted into the sandy, grass-tufted ground, and Hanna could see what an important position it had held. For a few minutes more she gazed at the river while Jay related historical facts as if he'd learned them from a textbook. He seemed to know a lot of local history, but then

Vicksburg was steeped in it and he must have heard about it from childhood. Then they went back to Aunt Rachael.

'Oh, it's lovely,' said Hanna. 'I wish you could have walked up there with us.'

'Perhaps I could have done if this had been an English climate,' her aunt said wistfully, and told Hanna how much better she was when it was cooler. But she loved America and wouldn't want to go back to England to live, even if the boys no longer needed her, so she supposed she would have to put up with the inconvenience of her unobliging legs and feet. Thank goodness her hands were not badly affected so she had no trouble playing Bridge, and was well able to cope with her various committees as long as someone was kind enough to take her along now that she was unable to drive.

On the way back they passed the Shirley House, which was the only surviving Civil War structure in the park. It had been restored to its original appearance, quite high on a green hillside.

'We've got an old print somewhere that shows that hillside pitted with caves and dugouts that they used for shelter during the Siege,' said Aunt Rachael. 'It's amazing the house survived at all.'

'If only it could talk, what a story it could tell,' said Hanna.

After lunch they drove down into the old part of the city, to the levee first so that Hanna could get a closer look at the river, and she was surprised to find it was only a quayside, though she was not sure what she had really expected. Next the antebellum houses, and Aunt Rachael was in her element talking about them. They were lovely, gracious buildings, mostly with wrought iron balustrades and steps leading up to handsome doors, but they were not as big as Hanna had thought they would be.

'Honey, you're getting confused with the plantation

houses like they have round Natchez. They were the great estates. These are elegant town houses.'

Jay took her into one of them. It was called Cedar Grove. The interior had been restored to its former beauty, magnificently furnished with upholstery in palest pinks and blues, mirrors from France, Chantilly porcelain, marble mantelpieces from Italy. General Grant once slept in one of the fourposter beds, and Jefferson Davis, the only President of the Confederacy, danced in the grand ballroom. There was even a cannonball embedded still in the parlour wall, a shot fired on the very first day of the Siege. Hanna was fascinated. And as she looked round the ballroom in particular, she was impressed by the accuracy of Ryan Donalson's interior scenes. *The Forty-seven Days* suddenly came to life for her.

Her aunt was getting tired. The strain showed in her eyes, though she tried hard not to show it, and towards the middle of the afternoon Hanna felt jet lag catching up with her and was able to plead tiredness herself quite truthfully.

'Perhaps we ought to make for home now, Jay,' said Aunt Rachael, and Jay headed out on the Port Gibson road after a short stop for cool drinks. On the way home they both told her snippets about Port Gibson, which had had its share of battles. There were some more antebellum houses, and a great number of churches, eight of them on Church Street. The one Hanna liked best had a gilded hand on top of the steeple pointing to heaven.

'There are chandeliers inside that came from the *Robert E. Lee* steamboat,' said Jay.

The Caldwells lived in a quiet road, and the house wasn't anything like Hanna had imagined. It was made of wood and there was a wide porch running the length of the front of the house which looked just the place for a rocking chair. There was no front garden, but a sweep of coarse grass down to the road. Front gardens, Aunt

Rachael said, were typically English. But surrounding the house were the most beautiful magnolia trees, their white, waxen blossoms fewer now than they had been a month earlier, but still lovely beside pink acacia trees and pecans.

It was cool indoors. The air-conditioning was on and the sun filtered through the prettiest white muslin curtains with frilled edges. The lounge was mostly green and white with a thick green carpet that was like soft, dark moss to tread on. Pictures of the English countryside were grouped on pastel green walls, and the long curtains were of the same delicate green. There were cushions on every chair in tones of green and palest yellow, but one thing caught Hanna's eyes before anything else. On a white table by the window there was a lamp with a white glass shade, and beside it in a shallow dish was a single white magnolia bloom, its petals curving outwards like a cluster of crescent moons. It was as big as a dinner plate and so beautiful it hardly seemed real.

All the rooms were on one floor and Hanna's bedroom faced the back garden, or yard as Aunt Rachael called it when she showed her in, though anything less like a back yard at home was hard to imagine. Another enormous magnolia tree dominated the piece of lawn and two more pecan trees gave a welcome stretch of shade. There was a patchwork quilt on her bed that Aunt Rachael had made in tones of pink and lilac, and once again the draped muslin curtains covered the windows. It was a lovely room, and she was glad when her aunt suggested she have a shower and rest quietly on the bed for a while.

Leigh came home early from college. Jay, it seemed, had taken the day off, but his brother was the studious one and hadn't thought it necessary to lose more than an hour's work. He was less exuberant than Jay but equally pleased to greet his cousin, and Hanna liked his quiet manner. He was the younger by two years, but could have been taken for older, and like Jay he obviously adored his mother. They both fussed over her, and Aunt Rachael accepted the attention happily whether it was necessary or not rather than hurt their feelings. She was justly proud of her sons.

The four of them had a meal at a restaurant which did barbecued food, and Hanna was overwhelmed by the amount on her plate, chicken, ham, beef and spare ribs all at at one serving being almost more than she could cope with, but she managed to work her way through to a dessert of fresh strawberries and cream. Eating was made more difficult by Aunt Rachael, who wanted to hear all the news from home at the same time, and the boys plied her with questions about England. But she enjoyed the evening immensely.

'How old are you now, Hanna?' Aunt Rachael asked. 'Twenty-one? It's high time you were thinking of marriage. Do you have a regular boy back home?'

'There was one once, but it wasn't serious enough. I haven't met anyone yet I'd like to marry.'

Her aunt toyed with a spoon in her coffee cup. 'How would you feel about living out here?'

Scheming, matchmaking Aunt Rachael! She hadn't waited five minutes before trying to get her interested in the boys, but though it was complimentary Hanna was not going to play along with that little game. 'I'll let you know when I've been here long enough to get used to the climate,' she laughed.

It was dark when they left the restaurant and still very hot, but it had started to rain. On the drive back it became a torrential downpour and the windscreen wipers were almost useless, but it didn't seem to bother Jay. Hanna was glad when they were home.

She was about to say goodnight and retire to bed when Jay called her.

'Come out here on the porch, Hanna, and watch the rain.'

Aunt Rachael had gone to bed, and Leigh was writing

up notes for college next day. The front door was open
to let in the night air, but there was a wire mesh door as
well to keep out insects and it slammed back on a spring
when she went outside.

'It won't thunder, will it?' she asked nervously.

He looked up at the sky. 'Not tonight.'

The temperature was still in the eighties, but rain fell
like a cascade and steam was rising from the hot, wet
earth. The shingled roof over the porch vibrated with
the deluge and the noise it made was like cracking fireworks. It was exciting. Hanna went and stood beside
her cousin and spray from the soaking grass splashed
up on her legs like a warm shower.

'See that hole over there,' said Jay. She looked to
where he pointed near the bottom step. 'That's where a
crawfish lives.'

The hole looked as if a walking stick could have been
pushed down to make it. 'But I always thought crawfish
lived in the sea.'

'Not this kind. He digs down till he finds water. Guess
he won't have much hard digging to do tonight!'

'I wish I could see him,' said Hanna.

'Perhaps he wishes he could see you. Any guy would,'
said Jay.

He was leaning on the porch rail and his eyes ap-
praised her. She smiled at him, responding with amusement to the flirtation in his tone. But seeing him standing there like that reminded her of Ryan Donalson. A
light through the window shone on Jay's hair, turning it
silver fair, and shadows accentuated the angular lines of
his face; but if she half closed her eyes and only focused
on his tall figure she could picture glistening brown curls
and an aquiline nose, craggy brows and a firm mouth.
When she thought of Ryan, Jay's youthful good looks
paled by comparison.

She wondered what Ryan's day had been like. It
seemed hours and hours since she had had breakfast
with him at the motel. Was he standing alone again on

that balcony tonight letting loneliness and heartache keep him awake? She hoped he wasn't. He seemed a long way away suddenly, and she reached out to him in her thoughts, strangely anxious for him to be happy.

CHAPTER SIX

'FOR God's sake get some more movement into it, and track back on that speech sooner,' Ryan shouted. 'These people have just been taken over by the Yankees. They're not going to stand there like dummies. I want to *see* their reaction.'

The scene outside the Old Court House was a dramatic interpretation of Vicksburg on the day the Siege was finally over, but by the frantic activity going on anyone would have been forgiven for thinking it had only just started. A United States flag was raised over the building and a Yankee General was addressing the crowd, mostly made up of women and children who had come out of hiding now the bombardment was over, old men and Confederate soldiers, some of them injured. The imposing collection of extras milled around amidst wires, lamps, rails for the camera to be moved backwards and forwards, cameramen, sound technicians, production assistants. And in the middle of it all Ryan Donalson made his presence felt. Not satisfied with the morning's progress, he was taking it out on cast and crew alike.

'Cut to the General's arrival again,' he yelled, striding down a grassy slope to where he had left a clipboard. 'Go back to where you were, all of you, and when you see him, shout! The cowed silence comes later.' He looked round, eagle-eyed, glaring above the heads. 'Where the hell is my script-writer?'

'It says a close-up of the General,' said Bill Hickly, flicking back pages without too much concern. 'Don't you want it that way now?'

'I want to *feel* the mood of the crowd. At the moment they could all be at a fair, and it won't do.'

Ryan turned to the actor taking the part of the General. 'Michael, you're supposed to be an actor. You're a General. You've taken this town after a siege lasting two bloody months. You're victorious. I want the camera focused on your back as you go up to the entrance, and you've got to make these people hate you by the very way you walk. Damn it, man, you don't just act with your face.'

'But that's not the way it is in the script,' the actor protested.

Ryan went over to Bill Hickly and together they went through directions, Ryan indicating positions he thought important. The crowd relaxed. A few sat on the grass, glad of hats and sunbonnets to shade their heads. And seeing their lethargy, Ryan yelled in exasperation: 'Okay, break for half and hour. After that I want it right. It's not a long scene. It ought to have been in the can by lunchtime, but at the rate we're going you'll all be here till nightfall!'

Hanna saw him as soon as she got out of the car at the edge of the cordon, and quailed inwardly. The absurd hope that he might not have missed her disappeared into the blue and she knew she was going to be at the receiving end of his wrath. It wasn't her fault she was late. Nor was it Jay's fault really. If that dreadful dog hadn't run into the road, making him brake sharply, she wouldn't have bumped her head, and all the trouble re-starting the car would have been avoided. As she approached the hub of activity she could see Ryan's thunderous expression and knew it was back to square one. He was still the objectionable, overbearing man she had met at Beauman Studios and disliked instantly.

The morning hadn't started too well. Neither of the boys was used to getting up early and to get Hanna into Vicksburg by eight o'clock meant breakfast by six-thirty. She was up before any of them, and it was she who took Aunt Rachael a cup of tea. When Jay appeared he was still half asleep, and even ice-cold fruit juice did little to revitalise him.

'Will you always be starting at this ungodly hour?' he asked, running his fingers through his thick golden hair, and yawning.

'Maybe even earlier,' Hanna teased.

'Oh, no! We'll have to hire you a car. I can't get up at this time every morning.'

She felt awkward. It was fine coming to visit relations, but not if they thought her a nuisance.

'Perhaps I could phone for a taxi,' she suggested. But Jay wouldn't hear of it. He put on a bright smile, poured milk over some breakfast cereal and sat on the edge of a stool.

'Cousin Hanna, for you I'll become a reformed man. I'll get up at the crack of dawn every day, and with you around I'm even gonna like it.'

Just before leaving the house she went into the lounge and the beautiful creamy white magnolia bloom in the glass dish had turned brown, just as if it was made of brown suede. She stared at it in disbelief, and somehow it made her sad. Nothing ever stayed the same, and it didn't seem right that such a lovely thing could change overnight into a dried shell that would break at a touch. Yet there was still loveliness in it. Like a broken love affair, the memory of how it had been was there. It made her think of Jessica taking the colour out of Ryan's life, turning it brown without warning, and she was full of sorrow for him. On impulse she went outside and picked a huge bud from the nearest magnolia tree, discarded yesterday's flower and filled the dish with fresh water. The pale bloom, washed by last night's rain, glowed with new beauty as the sun touched its uncurling petals, and only then did her spirits lift.

Strange how distance can mellow even the most difficult relationships. Last night and first thing this morning she had been quite kindly disposed towards Ryan, but the moment she came near him her nerves began to tingle. True she was over two hours late arriving and he would have every right to be cross, but knowing his irascibility when he was at work she was sure he would not have patience with excuses. And she was quite right.

'So you finally condescended to come,' he said scathingly.

'I'm sorry . . .' she began.

He looked at his watch, then rounded on Jay. 'I take it you can tell the time. What do you mean by keeping her this long?'

He was wearing khaki shorts, faded and well-worn, and she wondered where he had been to get his strong, muscular legs so brown. His bare feet were thrust into leather thongs and the collar of his white T-shirt was turned up to keep the sun off the back of his neck. Yet in spite of such casual attire his authoritative air was in no way diminished. Hanna felt out of place in a neat cotton sundress. Casualness applied to everyone where clothes were concerned, most of the men sporting baseball type hats which were almost regulation uniform among the Americans, and they all wore shorts.

'I can explain,' said Jay. 'The car . . .'

'Look here, I make it ten-thirty and I've been working since six. Shooting started at seven o'clock and I gave Hanna an hour's grace as this was her first morning. Excuses are not good enough. Time wasted is money wasted in this business, and I needed Hanna here.'

That was when she lost her temper. The man was a tyrant, and she couldn't allow him to get away with it.

'Please don't speak to my cousin like that,' she said. 'He's been put to a lot of inconvenience on our behalf, and damaged his car into the bargain, so a bit of politeness wouldn't come amiss.' She pushed back her hair angrily. 'And I wish you wouldn't say "look here". It sounds so rude!'

'I don't need a lesson in manners from you,' said Ryan, his eyes becoming dangerously hard. Jay, on the sidelines, waited uncomfortably for a slanging match to develop, but to his surprise there was a change of tactics. Ryan now saw the graze above Hanna's eye which her hair had been hiding, and his expression altered. He touched her forehead. 'How did you get this?'

She flinched. 'If you'd listened I've been trying to tell you. A dog ran practically under our wheels and when Jay braked hard I hit my head on the dashboard. It was nothing. More important was that the car wouldn't start again after that and he had to walk to the nearest garage which was miles away to get someone to come back and see to it. You're lucky we're here now.'

For a fraction of a second his fingers lingered near the graze, then he turned again to Jay. 'Why the hell wasn't she wearing a seat-belt?' he demanded. 'She could have been seriously hurt.'

'I never use one,' said Jay.

'Then it's time you did.' Ryan scooped up his clipboard and some papers and a khaki jacket from the wall where he had dumped them. 'That cut needs attention. We'll go back to the motel and get it bathed.'

He started to walk off. Hanna mimed a plea to Jay, hoping he would understand, and followed Ryan.

'While we're there I'll arrange for you to have your room again,' he called over his shoulder. 'I'm not having this fiasco repeated.'

'What did you say?' She stopped in her tracks.

'I said you will be sleeping at the motel from now on.'

She was outraged. 'I will do no such thing! Wait!' She stood there until he turned back and listened. 'I came out here to see my aunt. Whatever will she think if I tell her I can't stay with her after all? She'll be terribly upset.'

'I know, and I'm sorry, but think about it and you'll realise I'm right. It's too far for you to come from Port Gibson every morning.'

'I will not stay at the motel.' On principle she was not going to agree. 'What right have you to dictate where I spend my free time?'

Ryan paused, and a smile suddenly tipped up the corners of his mouth. 'Tut, tut, Miss Ballantyne, you didn't let me finish, did you?'

Jay looked from one to the other with a puzzled frown, sensing an undercurrent between them that went deeper than at first appeared, though the reason for it eluded him. It was not like an ordinary quarrel, but more a battle of wills. He caught Hanna's arm to gain her attention.

'Cousin Hanna, I guess he may be right. You need to be on the spot if you have to start work at seven, and I sure enough couldn't get you here by that time. Suppose I fetch you after college and take you home, then get you back here by nightfall? Momma will understand.' He faced Ryan. 'But I insist on seeing her in the evenings.'

'Of course,' said Ryan. 'I knew you were a man of sense. And Hanna will naturally have days off to spend with her aunt. That was what I was going to say.'

She felt as if she was being tossed about like a shuttlecock and her indignation grew, but as Jay had gone over to Ryan's side she had no more ground for argument. Had she known what extraordinary hours she was going to have to start work she would not have allowed anything he said to sway her. In another couple of months she could have afforded to come over here on holiday, and that would have been decidedly preferable.

'Perhaps if you two have decided what's best for me to do I can get on with some work without wasting any more time,' she said.

'We'll attend to that cut first,' said Ryan.

'It can wait until lunchtime. The skin is hardly broken.'

Again that aggravating smile. 'All head injuries should receive proper attention. Remember? I insist you come with me now, if you'll excuse us, Jay.'

'Why, sure.' Jay seemed very young against Ryan and he accepted the curt dismissal without question, but

Hanna resented it. That discourteous attitude was all very well for dealing with men who worked under him, but he was not going to treat Jay with such brusqueness and get away with it. She caught hold of her cousin's hand and gave it an affectionate squeeze, then reached up on tiptoe and kissed him.

'Thank you for everything, Jay. I'll look forward to this evening,' she said, with more emphasis than she would have dreamed of using earlier. And Jay rose to the occasion. Taking advantage of the unexpected opportunity, he did exactly as she had hoped and kissed her back with boyish enthusiasm before departing for a late start at college. That would show Ryan Donalson he was not so all-important! But the little scene she had acted out strictly for his benefit was wasted, for when she looked round he was already walking towards the cordon and the place where his car was parked.

He drove swiftly round the block to the motel and she grudgingly admitted to herself that he was a much better driver than Jay. If he had been at the wheel this morning there wouldn't have been any panic over the dog and all this fuss would have been avoided. Now he appeared to be in one of his fouler moods. Not once did he glance at her, neither did he speak.

It was quiet in Ryan's room. He closed the door behind them and the rest of the world was shut out, left to bake in the dusty morning heat while they faced each other in cool isolation. Being alone with him at his flat had not felt like this. There hadn't been the same kind of tension. He left her standing in the middle of the room while he went to the bathroom and ran the tap, and she was glad of even the briefest respite from him. His silence scared her more than any of his biting words, and every nerve in her body was on edge.

He had only occupied the room for two nights, yet already he had made it unmistakably his own. He must have been working either into the early hours, or at first light, because there were books and papers beside his

bed. The shirt he had worn yesterday was draped over
the armchair, the creases in it giving it an especial
quality, identifying with him because he had worn it
next to his skin and she had the strangest urge to touch
it. His shoes lay on their sides just as he had kicked
them off and bottles of aftershave and lotion were scattered on the white unit top near the mirror. It crossed
her mind that anyone married to him would have a very
untidy husband. His hairbrush, for some reason, was on
the table by the door, as if he had gone outside with it
and deposited it in the nearest place when he returned.
She leaned towards it, trailed her fingers over the bristles
which had brushed through his thick brown hair, and
the prickling against her fingertips sent a tingling sensation through her scalp. When she looked at her hand
there were two curly strands of hair clinging to her and
she gripped them into her palm.

The bed was not made. They had passed an open
door two or three rooms back where a girl was working,
so Ryan's must have been one of the last on her list. A
duvet was folded to one side and the crumpled sheet
and pillowcase still had the imprint of where he had
been lying. The sight of it filled her with curious fasci-
nation. What on earth was the matter with her? She
pictured him sleeping there, half closed her eyes and the
duvet became herself curled up beside him. Oh, no!

'Hanna, are you all right?'

His voice was sharp and her eyes flew open. She was
breathing fast, amazed at the extraordinary trick her
imagination had played, and her face coloured.

'I'm fine,' she said shakily.

In the few seconds it had taken her to absorb the
atmosphere of the room he had found antiseptic cream
and lint, and run hot water into the handbasin in the
bathroom.

'You look as if you had quite a shock this morning.'

'I did.' It was a truthful answer. Whatever would he
say if he knew she had just thought of herself sharing

his bed? Knowing him, he would probably find it highly amusing and suggest trying it for real. It wasn't likely he would let a chance like that slip by. Thank goodness he wasn't able to read her mind!

It was a very tiny bathroom and Ryan seemed to fill it. Hanna was not a small girl, but when she stood beside him her eyes were on a level with his chest.

'This is quite unnecessary,' she said, feeling a peculiar giddiness in the confined space, as if she was was going to fall against him. 'It's only a surface scratch.'

He lifted the heavy reddish-brown hair away from her forehead and she turned sideways so that he could see. And in the mirror she caught sight of the angry red mark where she had banged into the dashboard. Until then she had hardly been aware of it, but when he touched it with gentle fingers the blood thumped in her temples.

He applied warm water carefully and examined the extent of the damage. 'You've already disrupted our first day's filming, a very important day, I might add, with hired cameras and hired extras who have to be dressed and catered for and paid, so the scene has to be shot in the least number of hours. The idea of bringing you along was mine because I argued that money could be saved by having script alterations done on the spot. I do not expect to be proved wrong. And we can't afford the expense or inconvenience of having you ill for the rest of the time.'

'That's right, put all the blame on me for your mistakes!' She jerked her head away furiously. 'I've explained about the breakdown. I've apologised. What more can I do?'

'Perhaps the biggest mistake was bringing you at all.'

She gasped. 'How can you be such a hypocrite? You know I didn't want to come anyway.'

'Rubbish!'

'And let me tell you the main reason why I didn't want to come was because I didn't think I could possibly work with you even for a few days.'

'Up to this moment you haven't even started to work, so how can you judge?'

He went to put antiseptic cream on her forehead, but she couldn't bear him to touch her again and other than pushing past him there was nowhere she could move, so she tried to take a step back. In danger of losing her balance, she clutched wildly at the nearest thing behind her, which happened to be the shower curtains, and the next thing she knew she was lying in a damp patch on the floor of Ryan's shower unit. Surprise robbed her of further angry words and she glared at him open-mouthed before trying, and failing, to get to her feet on the slippery porcelain, but she was too humiliated to ask for help. Nor did he offer it, and the reason became clear when she saw how hard he was trying not to laugh. Finally it was too much for him and he burst out laughing, the happy sound without a hint of malice reverberating round the tiled walls, and it was infectious. A moment later Hanna was laughing, too, and the more she tried to stand up, the funnier it became, so she stayed where she was until Ryan held out both hands to her.

He drew her to her feet, and as she stepped on to firm ground his arms went round her. They had both been shaking with laughter, but now they were still. She felt as if she was suffocating, and tensed her body, determined to resist the sudden pulsing excitement that whipped through her. But one of his hands cupped the back of her head, drawing her ever closer until her face was against his chest and she could hear the way his heart raced. For a few magical seconds she nestled there, experiencing the most wonderful sensations in the world, and then he shattered it all by indirectly reminding her that this was nothing more than a game.

'Please, Hanna, don't give me any more frights.' His voice was still full of amusement. 'Jessica will never forgive me if I fail to get her secretary back all in one piece.'

She stiffened and pulled away from him, coming to her senses immediately. All he was really worried about was Jessica, and that put everything in proper perspective.

'Will you now allow me to start work?' she asked, with more coolness than she was feeling. 'There's no sense in wasting any more time when you keep reminding me how valuable it is.'

He mustn't see the effect he had had on her. Damn him! Her legs felt weak and there was a sort of constriction in her chest that made breathing laborious. What a fool she had made of herself! She had been so scornful of women who found him attractive, yet the slightest physical contact made her completely disorientated. She must be mad. There was nothing likeable about him, so why did she react in this deplorable way, as if seeking cheap excitement? It was never going to happen again.

She gathered together what shreds of dignity she could salvage and made an aloof exit, but not before she had seen an envelope on the writing table addressed to Mrs Jessica Kerby. It was written in the same bold hand that she had seen on the letter in Jessica's bedside drawer. Strange to see her married name. It must have come hard to Ryan to use it, and Hanna felt a tug at her heart. He had obviously been thinking about her. Was that what had made him in such a bad mood this morning? Jessica's impetuous marriage had caused enough heartache and confusion, and it worried Hanna more every day, though she couldn't understand why.

There was no chance to think any more about it that day, because as soon as she got back to the Old Court House she was plunged into work with a vengeance. Personal problems were put aside as Ryan dictated what he wanted done and she found herself rewriting parts of a scene that had seemed perfectly feasible when she had originally typed them for Jessica. If she had known then that she would be expected to make alterations out here on location she wouldn't have thought it possible, but as the day wore on she began to enjoy the work immensely. It was certainly a challenge, but the atmosphere was electric and after a while she became so absorbed she could see where adjustments needed making almost before she was told.

Everything about the scene excited her. What had seemed like chaos when she first arrived took on new meaning as she watched what they were doing and could see how weeks of planning had gone into it all. With so many people involved there was no room for dithering and she even began to have sympathy with Ryan's impatience. He was a perfectionist and expected everyone else to come up to the same standard.

At lunchtime she was pleased to meet up with Vicki again. She hardly recognised her. The sophisticated girl on the flight over had vanished and Vicki had become a working girl in pink shorts and white T-shirt with 'Beauman Studios' printed across the back. Her hair was tied in a ponytail which made her seem much younger, and she wore an enormous pair of red sunglasses. The seven o'clock start Ryan had spoken of had been no exaggeration. Vicki and two other girls had worked since long before that, kitting out the extras in costumes which they had sorted and labelled the day before. It made Hanna feel guilty about having had the whole day off.

Coaches were used for catering and Vicki and Hanna collected hamburgers and Coke and took them to a shady spot where they could sit down.

'I don't know how they got everything organised so quickly,' said Hanna. 'If it was me I'd have had to spend days setting it all up.'

Vicki laughed. 'That's the unit manager's job. He came over at the beginning of the week and got everything organised, hired extras and another two cameras, made arrangements with the authorities for filming permission. I expect he even opened a bank account, so there's money available. It doesn't just happen automatically.'

'No, of course not.' Hanna bit thoughtfully into her hamburger. 'What about all these Civil War costumes? Where did they come from?'

'They were hired as well.'

'And how long will they all be needed?'

'Only today,' said Vicki. 'The really big scenes like this are done all in one go if possible, otherwise the cost would be too great. There's another one scheduled for next week when we film in the National Military Park, but this one is probably the most important. This afternoon they'll use the same people, but move them over to the other side of the Court House. It seems as if there are far more than there really are when it's all put together.'

Hanna had always taken television very much for granted, but now that she was involved she wanted to learn everything she could about it and she plied Vicki with questions which she tried her best to answer.

'Those are the generators over there,' she said, pointing across to the green slopes in front of the Old Court House. 'That spark's just going over to one.'

'Spark? Isn't that dangerous?'

'No, silly. A spark is what we call an electrician,' Vicki explained. 'The generators provide electricity for those lamps on the stands.'

'But why do they have lamps out of doors? Surely it's bright enough without, especially here.'

'Not for filming.' She went on to tell her as much as she knew about it, then changed the subject to something which interested her far more. 'Tell me, who was that gorgeous feller you were with this morning? Friend Ryan looked as if he could have killed him.'

'That's my cousin,' Hanna laughed. 'He is rather sweet, isn't he?'

'Sweet! What an understatement.' Vicki cast her a sidelong glance, full of speculation. 'Ryan isn't used to competition. It should be good for him.'

'What do you mean by that?'

'It hasn't gone unnoticed that he singles you out for special attention,' said Vicki.

Hanna's cheeks burned and she resented the implication that Ryan was showing favouritism. She didn't want her name linked with his in any way.

'It's only because of my connection with Jessica. I assure you he isn't the slightest bit interested in me otherwise, and I certainly don't want him to be. We haven't anything in common. In fact he infuriates me.' She was being over-emphatic, but she had to dispel any wrong ideas straight away.

Vicki shrugged her shoulders. 'I hope you're right. You can't expect to attract *all* the talent.'

At that Hanna giggled like a schoolgirl. She had never considered herself anything out of the ordinary, and the idea of Vicki being worried about competition was the funniest thing out.

'With you around I wouldn't even try,' she said good-humouredly.

If Vicki hoped to get Ryan Donalson on the rebound she was welcome. Hanna's greatest wish was to avoid him.

She was nowhere near ready when Jay came for her late in the afternoon, but he was as fascinated with all that was going on as she had been and was quite happy to wait. By the time Ryan said he wouldn't be needing her any more that day the scene looked more like the aftermath of a school outing and she was glad she didn't have to stay behind and help to clear it up. She was tired, which was not surprising, and her exasperation over the move back to a motel room had subsided. She would have welcomed a quiet hour to herself instead of having to drive all the way back to Port Gibson.

Jay kept up a steady stream of inconsequential chatter as they drove along and she let it drift over her head, hoping she was making the right answers. It was as if he were nervous. She half-closed her eyes, aware that he kept looking at her, and she smiled, remembering Vicki's comment. Perhaps it was her English accent that attracted him. Whatever it was there was no doubt she had made a conquest, and while it was flattering she knew she would have to be careful not to give him any more encouragement like that little episode this morning. He would be rightfully angry if he knew that she had played him off against Ryan Donalson.

As Hanna had expected, Aunt Rachael was very disappointed when she heard about the move back to the motel.

'I'd like to give that Mr Donalson a piece of my mind,' she said. But luckily she was a philosophical person and had to agree that it was a more sensible arrangement. 'I suppose I can't monopolise you when your firm are paying expenses. I'm just so glad they made it possible for you to come. Tell you what, honey, maybe when they go back you could stay on with us for a day or two longer. I'm sure they wouldn't mind.'

Hanna gave her a swift hug. 'Thank you. That would be lovely.' But she was none too sure it would be possible. She had already come away without Jessica's knowledge or permission and it was imperative that she should arrive back at the same time as the Beauman Television Company. However, she would talk it over with her aunt later on and perhaps plan a date for her to come over on holiday at the end of the summer.

'I bet Jay heaved a sigh of relief now he won't have to keep getting up at an ungodly hour,' said Leigh.

'He didn't mind at all,' Aunt Rachael said quickly.

Leigh chuckled. 'He'll do anything to impress a beautiful girl except get up early. He sure must be struck on you to have done it this morning.'

'What's that?' Jay had come in from the kitchen and heard them joking.

'Your brother's jealous, son,' his mother said. 'He was going to offer to drive Hanna into Vicksburg at six o'clock tomorrow.'

'I was not,' Leigh protested, and everyone laughed.

'Anyway, I saw her first,' said Jay. He slipped an arm round her waist with a proprietorial air, and she hadn't the heart to let them see she didn't want that kind of attention. They were a naturally demonstrative family and their kindness touched her deeply. She even let Jay drop a kiss on her cheek without drawing away.

Next evening he took her on the river.

After a meal at a seafood restaurant in town they went down to the water front, boarded a motor vessel and found a seat in the bows where she would be able to see everything. He had warned her not to expect a romantic river boat, but she assured him any kind of boat would do as long as it took her on a trip down the Mississippi. Before going up the gangway she trailed her hand in the water, much to Jay's amusement. He failed to see what was so wonderful about the muddy old river he had known all his life.

'It's just a strip of water the same as any other.'

'No, it's not. Even the name is exciting. It's got a sort of magic.'

'You're crazy,' he teased. 'There's a saying that it's too thick to drink and too thin to plough. Nothing magic about that.'

Vicksburg looked good from the river and she could see why they had been able to defend it so well when gunboats attacked. It was built on a hill commanding views in either direction so that no shipping could approach without warning, and steep streets climbed up to historic landmarks like the Old Court House and the Christ Episcopal Church as well as new blocks of flats and offices. They cruised up the Yazoo River, past the sad, burnt-out shell of the largest sternwheeler towboat ever to ply the Mississippi and which Jay said was called the *Sprague*, then turned and headed out into the wide Mississippi River itself. By then it was dark and the moon was making a broad pathway across the water, like liquid silver, and Hanna was enchanted. She leaned over the rail, wishing everyone else would go away so that she could be alone to absorb the beauty of it all.

And yet now there was nothing to see. On either side the river bank was only a smudge of endless trees, and a gentle breeze barely ruffled the surface of the water. She tried to close her ears to the quiet music in the background which she considered unnecessary, but somehow the strains of 'Moon River' being played unobtrusively against such a setting touched her emotions and she could have cried with happiness.

'It's so lovely, Jay. I wouldn't have missed this for anything. Thank you for bringing me.'

The breeze became cooler as the boat turned, and they were strolling down towards the covered deck. Jay caught hold of her arm, drawing her near him, and before they got too close to a little knot of passengers by the bar entrance, he stopped.

'*You're* lovely, Hanna, like that beautiful siren who was supposed to lure all men to her.'

'That was the Lorelei, and she lured them to their doom,' Hanna laughed. 'I hope I never do that.'

He swung round to face her, his arms encircling her waist, and she was too surprised to escape.

'Stop kidding, please. I'm serious. I'm in love with you.'

He bent his head and brought his mouth down hard on hers, and for a moment she could do nothing to avoid his masterful kissing. She made no response and waited for the opportunity to break away so that she could tell him as kindly as possible it was not what she wanted, but just as she was making a desperate effort to free herself, someone pushed past, separating them anyway.

'You're blocking the gangway,' a voice said—a deep, cultured, very English voice that was all too familiar. It was Ryan Donalson. He didn't look round or appear to recognise the couple who had inconvenienced him, and Hanna watched his progress along the deck, mesmerised and filled with trepidation. What if he had known who it was and not said? She couldn't bear it. The pressure of Jay's arms round her had hurt, but the ache that spread upwards from her toes had nothing to do with Jay.

'Hanna,' he said, trying to regain her attention.

'Please, Jay, don't do that again. We're cousins. Let's just keep it casual.'

Her eyes were on Ryan still. He was carrying two full glasses which he took over to a girl in pink trousers and sweater, and when she flicked aside a tangle of fair hair Hanna saw it was Vicki.

For a few seconds she closed her eyes so tight there was a pain behind them that effectively blotted out the picture of Ryan and Vicki together, then she turned her back on them and tried to concentrate on what her cousin was saying.

CHAPTER SEVEN

RYAN was not down for breakfast next morning; neither was Vicki. Hanna tried not to turn her head every time the door opened, because she didn't want to see them come in together.

She was not hungry. It was as much as she could do to swallow coffee and a bread roll, and she hadn't joined the group of girls she was with yesterday for breakfast because she couldn't face holding a conversation. Everything seemed to have changed, even the weather. Rain was cascading down the windows and it looked as if the grey sky was never going to show blue again.

She tried telling herself it was Jay's fault she was so desolate. He had ruined the evening with his intensity, and though she tried her best to persuade him he was not in love with her he was still boringly ardent by the time they got back to the motel, and she only just managed to avoid being kissed again.

'I don't understand you,' he kept saying. 'Out there by the Court House you showed you cared about me, right there in front of that guy Donalson. Now you make out that it was cousinly affection and I imagined things. Well, it's not a juvenile crush I've got. I really do love you.'

Hanna felt terribly guilty and wished she had never given him that first bit of encouragement, but how was she to know he was going to take it seriously? She hated hurting him, but he would soon get over it when she returned to England. Meanwhile she had to tread extra carefully from now on so that he wouldn't read any more hidden promises into her actions. She was sure she could cope with him and keep him safely at arm's length. It was her reaction to Ryan Donalson that really worried her.

The truth of it was her evening had not been ruined by Jay's declaration of love so much as by the fear of Ryan bumping into them a second time and recognising her. She couldn't bear to think of the mockery there would have been in his eyes when he realised she and Jay were the couple he had interrupted kissing in public like a couple of adolescents. Nor had she wanted to meet Vicki with Ryan, triumphant at having hooked him.

Hanna's spirits were at a low ebb. Jay had said she was lovely, but she knew she couldn't hold a candle to Vicki when it came to style. Vicki had flair, a distinctive way of wearing clothes so that it didn't matter whether they were expensive or not, a provocative tilt to her head, a sexy walk. Men noticed her—like Ryan. Beside her Hanna felt positively old-fashioned and knew it was time she did something about it.

She crumbled the roll on her plate absentmindedly, and tried to examine her feelings. It sounded as if she was trying to compete with Vicki and there could only be one reason for doing that: jealousy. She lifted her chin in defiance. What a ridiculous notion! Why should she envy her anything, particularly her friendship with Ryan, if that was what was at the bottom of it? What they did was none of her business, and the sooner she stopped thinking about them the better.

She went up to her room, having checked with Bill Hickly that filming would be delayed until the rain stopped. The schedule had been for location work outside the Balfour House, a relatively small scene which was not likely to take more than half a day anyway, and it was hardly likely she would be needed. She had a portable typewriter on loan in her room and notes she was making for Jessica's benefit, so she decided to get them up to date before going downstairs again. But she was too restless to concentrate. After spoiling the second sheet of paper she gave up and went to the wardrobe to get her raincoat. Perhaps the rain would wash away her depression.

Before going out she counted her traveller's cheques and found she was well within her spending limit and could afford to buy herself something new. She wished Vicki had been around to come with her, but there was still no sign of her anywhere, and she didn't know the other girls well enough to invite them, so she had to go alone. Shopping was not quite the same as at home. After enquiring at Reception, she called a taxi that took her out to the nearest shopping mall, and there she spent an hour browsing through open-fronted stores all under one roof. She bought a pair of tight white jeans, a jacket, a man's white shirt which was baggy on her but looked fabulous when drawn in with a red patent leather belt, red high-heeled sandals, and a wide-brimmed sunhat into which she could tuck her hair. Two more sun tops to go with the jeans and she had spent as much as she dared, but the spending spree had done wonders for her morale.

When she left the mall, the rain had stopped. She looked about her, trying to locate the nearest phone booth, and steam rose from the tarmac as it dried in the heat. Beads of perspiration collected under the hair on her forehead, and a neon sign outside the gas station across the car park recorded the temperature as a hundred and two degrees. Loaded with parcels and almost melting, Hanna thought it would be better to find a telephone inside the mall where it was cool, and she had just turned to retrace her steps when a car splashed to a stop beside her.

'Who the hell gave you permission to go out shopping this morning?' Ryan demanded, leaning out of the window. His scowl was darker than the clouds now veering away across the Lousiana side of the river.

'I asked Bill Hickly. He said nothing could be done until the rain stopped.'

'And I suppose you knew exactly when that would

be. *Your* job isn't governed by the weather. I thought you'd have sense to realise a wet morning is the only time I get for paper work.'

'I'm *not* your secretary,' Hanna reminded him.

She was furious. He had obviously checked up on her with Reception, found out where she had gone and followed, then he had sat there in the car park like a cat waiting to pounce the moment she came into the open.

'Get in,' he said. The car was too wide for him to lean over and open the door for her, and it was tempting to refuse, but at least she would get a free ride back to the motel and it would save waiting for a taxi. Besides, that scowl showed no sign of lifting and this was no place for a showdown.

He eased out into the freeway and headed back to town, but instead of going to the motel he drove up the hill towards the National Military Park.

'Why didn't you wait for me this morning?' he asked. 'You might have known I'd want to see you.'

'I thought you were still with Vicki.'

The moment the words were out she regretted them, but she had merely continued her train of thought. She hadn't meant them to sound the way they did, accusing, laden with undertone. Ryan didn't take his eyes off the road, and she held her breath. He would either take the comment at face value, a casual remark as the result of a casual enquiry, in which case his answer depended on his involvement. Or he would know she had seen him last night and accuse her of nosing into his private affairs. She waited, not daring to look at him, and the moment passed without any reply at all. It felt as if a weight had been lifted from her.

He drove into the Military Park, showed his Press pass card and was allowed through. She didn't ask why they had come, or why he hadn't gone straight back to the motel if his paper work was so important. He never did anything without a reason. It was the first time she had been back since her day with Jay and Aunt Rachael, and she was glad to see it again. It was a haunting place that had had quite an impact on her, and being here with Ryan added a new dimension. Without a word being said, she knew his feelings for it went even deeper than her own.

There was no one about. The early rain had kept visitors away and the ghosts of bygone battles were undisturbed except for themselves. Hanna wished they were on foot instead of in the car so that she could have stood silently and listened to the true tales the park had to tell, though judging by all she had read and pictures she had seen it was doubtful whether she could have listened for long without covering her ears. The car crept past monuments and marker-dotted hillsides, Ryan making no effort at conversation, and presently he drew up on the brow of a hill that sloped away down to the right. He got out and walked to the edge. Hanna followed, having first removed the sunhat from its wrappings, twisted her hair into a knot and bundled it into the crown as she pushed the hat down on her head.

'Seventeen thousand Yankee soldiers died trying to capture Vicksburg,' Ryan said. 'A lot died in a ghastly battle on this hill that lasted for days, and it was so hot they had to call a truce in the middle of it so they could bury the dead.'

He didn't say why he was telling her about it and she gazed down the gentle, grassy slope, trying to visualise the picture he painted. He was remote, hardly aware of her presence, and as he talked about it she could see him reliving it mentally. He was suffering with men who had suffered unbelievably on this spot. How different from Jay's attitude, his remark that he guessed they had had a pretty rough time.

'I can see the appalling bloodshed, all the horror of battle at such close quarters,' he went on. 'Jessica's script dealt with it superbly. But why hasn't she shown the tragedy of it? I want to capture the pathos.' He shut his eyes, as if to re-focus, then turned to Hanna. 'Can *you* understand there is a difference?'

'Yes,' she said, without hesitation, 'I can.' But it was a minute or two before she could form her reasons. A memory played elusively at the back of her mind like a shadow dance, and she groped for it. Something he had said on the drive through from Jackson. 'Fraternisation.' She paused again, thoughtfully. 'The scene where Linderley's brother is wounded . . .'

Linderley was not the main character in *The Forty-Seven Days*, but she had always been more real to Hanna than the rich heroine in her beautiful antebellum house. Linderley went to live in a cave on the hillside below the Shirley House with her family to shelter from the bombardment, but she had attended to the wounded and attended to the necessities of everyday life fearless of the shelling. She was one of the heroic young women of Vicksburg, but the secret she guarded was her love for a Yankee infantryman whom she had known since childhood. He was the same age as her brother, and it was he who found her brother badly injured and left for dead.

'Go on,' Ryan prompted, now giving her all his attention.

'You remember saying the lines were so close they could talk to each other? Well, I think those two boys could meet and talk the night before the battle . . .'

'On the day of the truce,' Ryan interrupted eagerly. He had seen the direction she was leading and took over. 'Flags went up all along the lines, and the troops had three hours' respite. They talked and laughed, believe it or not, and the Rebels gave the Confederates food and liquor.'

'No,' she said. 'It must be at night when it's quiet. They're both on picket duty and meet between the lines.'

'Night time, of course,' he agreed. 'You *have* got the feel for it. I knew I was right to bring you here. I'm not a writer. I know what I mean, but I can't always get

Jessica to see it. I want a very small scene written in. Can you do it?'

'I'd like to,' said Hanna.

Standing there beside him she felt very close to breaking through the confusion in her heart. An inner voice called out in recognition of like emotions and she longed for him to talk seriously of things that affected themselves. But he was too absorbed with the past, not separating her from it but drawing her into his passionate feeling for events that happened here over a hundred years ago.

'There are too many ghosts here, Hanna,' he sighed. Then he gave a half laugh which broke the spell, and went back to the car. This time he opened the door for her. 'I like the hat. It does things for you.'

Hanna flushed with pleasure and kept the hat on when she had been about to drag it off and shake her hair free.

He drove on round the park and she relaxed a little. He had asked her to do something specific which would add a touch of realism to *The Forty-seven Days*, and ensure she had really had a hand in it. He had faith in her capabilities and she forgot how agitated he had made her earlier. But she was soon reminded.

On a bluff above the river Ryan stopped again and leaned his arms nonchalantly over the steering wheel. For a while he said nothing, but a small, aggravating smile tipped his lips which she had come to recognise as trouble.

'Do you often come and admire the view?' she asked in a sharper tone than necessary because she had a premonition he was about to revert to character.

'No.' He moved his head sideways so that it was resting on his arms, and his eyes were on her. 'I thought you might like to look at the river properly as you didn't get a chance to see much of it last night.'

Hanna's heart took a swallow-dive and her mouth went dry. She might have known those penetrating brown eyes missed nothing. Yet why on earth was she worrying when all he had seen was Jay kissing her? So what! She had as much right to be kissed as anybody and didn't have to make any excuses or apologies. She licked her dry lips and lifted her chin the way she always did when it looked as if her integrity might be threatened.

'I had a wonderful evening,' she said. 'And I saw as much of the river as I could in the dark. No doubt you did, too.'

'It gets monotonous after a while,' he told her.

'I didn't find it so.'

'I'm sure you didn't. Luckily there were other distractions.' The cynical tone emphasised a double meaning and her temper flared.

'If you're referring to my being with Jay why don't you say so instead of making snide remarks? I enjoyed being with my cousin, and *I've* nothing to hide.'

'It wouldn't matter to me if you had,' he said, straightening his broad shoulders and stretching his arms, his hands still on the wheel. 'And as to the remark *you* made earlier, if you were implying that I slept with Vicki Lander perhaps you'll be good enough to mind your own business.'

The attempt to put her in her place almost succeeded. She knew she had no right to criticise him, but it wasn't all one-sided and some demon led her on. She couldn't let him get away with it.

'How do you know what was meant unless you have a guilty conscience. I don't care what you do to get Jessica out of your system as long as you don't involve me.'

'Leave Jessica out of it.'

The words stabbed at her like cold steel, and before she could say anything else he started the car. She had raised her voice, but his remained dangerously on one level and she took it as a warning not to let the bitter words develop into a full-scale row. Why had this angry exchange started anyway, when only a few minutes before they had been so unusually in tune? She couldn't understand it.

The sun broke through, painting golden flecks on the distant water, and a convoy of barges was pushed by a tug into a shaft of sunlight like stage illumination. Ryan paused, struck by the beauty that had appeared from nowhere.

'That's fantastic,' he said. 'Those barges look like a fat little chorus. You know, I couldn't have done it better myself.'

The transition from storm to sunshine, both actually and metaphorically, took her quite by surprise while her vision was still blurred by emotion. Then she saw what he meant and gave an explosive little giggle.

'I always knew you were conceited,' she said, 'but that takes some beating!'

The incident cleared the atmosphere temporarily and the drive back to the motel was bearable. But she was not at ease with him. She gave a sigh. He was one of those people it was impossible to get along with, and the more she tried the more difficult it was. There was something about him that made sparks fly when she came too close, a high voltage antagonism that brought out the worst in her. She sat very straight in her seat, nose in the air, chin held high, and the wide-brimmed hat with all her hair tucked inside lent a pose of wounded dignity which, had she been able to see, caused him much secret amusement. The hat brim formed a sort of barrier. With her head slightly tilted she couldn't see him, and that was the way she wanted it.

He dropped her at the motel entrance.

'Lunch,' he said, 'then the Balfour House this afternoon. I don't anticipate making any changes, but you'd better be there. Get Bill Hickly, or one of the boys to drive you over. Oh, and this evening I shall want you with us when we see the rushes of the Old Court House scene.'

'This evening?'

She was on the pavement and his curt instructions were no more than she expected, so she was already turning away when she caught the final sentence.

'That's right. We've rented a small studio and I'll be over there going through the rushes most evenings.'

'But do you really need me there?'

'Among others, yes.'

She wondered if he was doing it deliberately. 'You could have given me more warning,' she said. 'Jay was going to take me back to Port Gibson to be with Aunt Rachael.'

'I'm sorry,' said Ryan offhandedly. 'You'll just have to contact him.'

He drove off without another word, away from the motel, his destination undisclosed, and Hanna gritted her teeth because she felt almost at screaming pitch. He was probably going to meet Vicki somewhere for lunch. Perhaps it would improve his mood.

But Hanna's mood remained curiously disturbed and she found she was still not hungry even though she had gone without breakfast. She put it down to the fact she was not used to such a hot climate and had eaten far more than she normally did since she had been here. A glass of tonic water in the bar and a sandwich was all she could manage, then she went up to her room and tried on her new clothes. By tilting the dressing-table mirror she could get a full-length view of herself and she tried a few experimental poses to get the best effect. Her slim body looked good in the jeans and she decided her hips were not so wide as Vicki's, which was consoling. The white top with fine red stripes teamed up well, and she slipped her feet into the red sandals, wriggling her toes experimentally to make sure they were comfortable. Lastly she coiled her hair and pinned it into a topknot.

'Hanna Ballantyne, you don't look at all bad,' she told herself. 'What's Vicki Lander got that you haven't?'

And the answer came back immediately, making her wilt. 'For one thing, she's got Ryan Donalson.'

It was such a stupid thing to care about. What did it matter if the two of them had paired up? Someone was bound to step into Jessica's shoes sooner or later and it might just as well be Vicki. So why did the thought of them together keep nagging at her constantly?

She decided to wear her new things. They might give her some badly needed confidence.

There was no sign of Vicki after lunch, and Ryan was too involved with technical problems to seek out Hanna. It was a long, tedious afternoon and she was glad when everyone packed up, apparently satisfied with results after what had sounded like an unsatisfactory few hours re-taking shots. She had tried to understand what made them good or bad, but it was all too complex.

It was the last week of term at Jay's college and when she tried to contact him at a number he had given her she was told he had left early, so she couldn't let him know she had to work late. She was worried what he would say. He would think she had done it on purpose to avoid being with him and it would be a job to convince him otherwise. It also meant she would have to eat at the motel. The answer, of course, was to phone Aunt Rachael and explain.

'I'm so sorry,' she apologised. It was so nice to hear the warm affection in her aunt's voice that a huge wave of self-pity welled up in her without warning and she felt on the verge of tears. 'Everything seems to be going wrong. I thought I was going to see such a lot of you and I've hardly seen you at all.'

'Don't worry, honey,' said Aunt Rachael. 'We'll make up for it later. That big boss of yours sounds like a real slavedriver. Just you bring him over here so I can give him a piece of my mind!'

The thought of her diminutive aunt intimidating Ryan was quite something and it made Hanna laugh. 'I believe you would, too.'

'Just so long as you're able to go with Jay to his end of term dance, Hanna,' she said, more seriously. 'He'll be a mite disappointed if you don't.'

'It's tomorrow night, isn't it? I'll be there for sure. I brought an evening dress with me.'

There was a note for Hanna when she went for her key at Reception. She unfolded it and saw Ryan's bold scrawl across the paper. 'We'll pick you up here at eight o'clock. Ryan.'

She didn't change for dinner. There was no point. This time she joined the other girls, knowing it would be no good watching the door for Ryan and Vicki because they would be having a cosy meal alone somewhere. Hanna had torn the note in half and thrown it in the wastepaper basket.

She was waiting for them promptly at eight, tendrils of hair that had come lose from the topknot escaping over her ears and forehead, and the white jacket was over her shoulders. Ten minutes later they arrived and she was trying not to tap her sandalled feet impatiently.

'We're late, Hanna, I'm sorry,' said Ryan, hurrying up the steps. 'You could have gone on with Bill and the others.'

'Your note said you would pick me up,' she reminded him.

'All right then, let's get on.' He turned to Vicki who was just behind him, and his voice softened. 'Vicki, thank you for everything. You've been marvellous. I'll see you in the morning.'

'Thank you, too,' said Vicki. 'And, Ryan, don't work too late. See that he doesn't, won't you, Hanna?'

Hanna kept her eyebrows straight with difficulty, resisting the temptation to raise them. She was embarrassed. Vicki had made a conquest, but there was no need to flaunt it openly, and Hanna was not going to give her the satisfaction of letting her see it meant anything. Not that it did anyway, she told herself firmly.

She found she was in glamorous company on the

journey over to the studio. The leading actor and actress shared Ryan's car. She was not included in the conversation except for a few cursory questions from the actress who sat beside her in the back seat and felt obliged to be polite, and Hanna was glad. She didn't want to speak to anyone, particularly Ryan, while her thoughts were in such chaos. Nothing made sense. She had liked Vicki Lander and they had got on well, so why did she suddenly resent her, as if she had changed?

The gravel-covered parking lot behind the studio was full of waterlogged potholes from the morning rain. Ryan got out first and waited for Hanna who was replacing the jacket which had slipped from her shoulders. The others went on ahead.

'Mind where you tread,' he warned, and as she went to step out of the car one of the backless sandals dropped from her foot. He stooped to retrieve it while she was still sitting there and held it out on the palm of his hand, a warm smile lighting his eyes. 'I know I'm not your Prince Charming, and though you look stunning in that outfit it's hardly Cinderella, but allow me to try on this glass slipper.'

He was crouching in front of her, looking up, and he took hold of her foot very gently. For a moment he held it cupped in his palm and moved his thumb along the instep in the most sensual way, causing an exquisite pleasure to surge through her. Their eyes met. She was captive for several breathless seconds, oblivious of time or place, and only by a supreme effort did she stop herself holding out her arms to him. He put the shoe on.

'It fits, Hanna,' he said softly.

With a little gasp she arched her foot and drew it away.

In the protective darkness of the studio she tried to concentrate on the strip of film being given a trial run, knowing she was there to concentrate on its quality and correctness, but the fire Ryan had kindled would not be quenched and it affected her judgment so that she could see only the brilliance of his work and not a single fault. Having watched the scene being shot she marvelled at the depth it contained, the atmosphere, the conflicting reactions of the people from fierce resentment to relief that the Siege was over. It was all there, and she was full of admiration. But more than that she was completely preoccupied by the way she suddenly felt about Ryan himself.

She was sitting in front of him and daren't turn her head in case their eyes should meet again. He was too powerful. All he had to do was look at her and she went to pieces, and a single touch made her limbs feel as if they didn't belong to her. No one else had ever made her feel like this. Whatever she might think of him as a person made no difference to the primitive need he had awakened in her, and his physical attraction could not be ignored. She had fought against it, but the battle was lost—had been lost before it had hardly begun. She didn't like him, yet the force of his personality sent shock waves through her and when he was near it was as if everyone else faded into anonymity. There was only one explanation, whether she liked it or not. She wanted him. No good hiding behind discreet phrases, though she was dismayed by the discovery.

She had thought she was immune to that vital, inexplicable magnetism which she had privately ridiculed, but it had proved to be too strong. In the darkness she relived the way Ryan had held and kissed her that night in his flat and knew if it happened again she wouldn't even try to resist. Just thinking about it filled her with strange excitement, like pins and needles all over her skin, but it changed to pain when she remembered it was Vicki who had captured all his attention.

Why couldn't she have felt this way about Jay, who was her own age? She was genuinely fond of her cousin and liked being with him, and she hadn't wanted to hurt him. If only she could have fallen in love with him it would have made both her mother and Aunt Rachael very happy, but there was no way she could feel anything other than affection for him. She might have mistaken that affection for something more if this new phenomenon hadn't burst upon her. There was nothing to compare with the hunger that gripped her, hunger that had nothing to do with food except that she couldn't face any. Only one man could produce this breath-stopping emotion which kept her in a state of turmoil, and that was Ryan. Ryan, who was at least fourteen years older than she, clever, celebrated, sought after, way beyond her reach. What a mess she was in.

Instinct told her that Ryan was not totally oblivious to the situation. There were times when attraction sparked between them like forked lightning and always ended in thunderous words because agreement was impossible while they were fighting baser problems. Knowing him, she was pretty sure he must have considered her for a one-night stand at least, and might even suggest it if the opportunity arose. Perhaps he was saving it until he grew tired of Vicki. It just went to show what a low opinion she had of him, and yet if such an opportunity *did* arise she was frightened to think of her reaction. In all her life she had never been in such a dilemma. The only way was to steer well clear of him, but she had intended doing that from the beginning and look what had happened.

His eyes were on her. She could feel those keen, penetrating brown eyes burning into her and felt as if she was suffocating. She turned her head. His lips moved very slightly at the corners, his gaze didn't waver and he held her for several seconds by an invisible thread she was powerless to break.

Jay was waiting at the motel. He had been there all evening and his frustration could hardly be contained. It was such a relief to see him after the agonising time at the studio, and Hanna hurried to his side with a smile which cleared his angry scowl momentarily.

'Didn't you get my message, Jay? I phoned the college,

and I phoned your mother.'

'Yes, I got the message,' he said. 'I came to see why you're expected to be available even in your free time. We were told you could spend the evenings with us.' He was being almost petulant, like a small boy.

'It's part of my job, and in this job there are no set hours. Please understand,' she said, and was surprised at herself for supporting Ryan's request that she be there when the rushes were shown, when previously she had been as cross as Jay. She was rapidly becoming part of the company instead of an outsider, and to pacify him she went on: 'But don't worry, nothing will stop me being with you tomorrow evening.'

His face brightened. 'I'm counting on you. We're going to really live it up, sweetie.'

She didn't like being called 'sweetie' and the thought of living it up with Jay didn't appeal to her particularly, but she had to pretend for his sake. 'I'm looking forward to it,' she said.

'You can tell your big boss you've got a date tomorrow you can't break.'

'Why not tell me yourself?' said Ryan.

There was silence. Hanna hadn't seen him come in and the now recognisable pattern of quickened heartbeats and weakened limbs assailed her. His face was stony. That air of compelling authority was meant to be intimidating and she was afraid Jay would succumb to it, but he didn't.

'Hanna is my partner at the college dance tomorrow night,' he said, meeting Ryan's eyes with commendable self-confidence. 'I'd be obliged if you don't find work to keep her late again like tonight.'

Ryan showed no sign of temperament. He merely considered for a moment, then said: 'No problem. You can take Hanna back to Port Gibson tonight and she can have tomorrow off. I shan't be needing her until the day after.' He started to walk away, but added as an afterthought, 'You can write that scene we talked about,

Hanna, if you have the time.'

They stared after him, too surprised to answer, then Jay let out a whoop of joy. 'Yow-ee!' he cried, swinging her round. 'You're all mine for the next twenty-four hours!'

She freed herself hurriedly, embarrassed by the way people turned to look. And she was fuming. Ryan Donalson was the absolute limit, speaking about her as if she was part of the furniture, so offhand those intimate looks might never have passed between them. It just proved he wasn't the faintest bit interested in her, and would probably be glad when she was out of the way. What a fool she was, what a stupid fool, to let him walk over her. He wasn't worth the agony she was going through.

'I'll go up and get a few things,' she said to Jay, coolly. 'Wait here.'

She ought to have been thrilled at having a whole day and two nights free to spend with Aunt Rachael and her cousins. She'd lamented enough that there was no time to be with them. But suddenly the thought of not seeing Ryan for all those hours was unbearable, and all her fine resolutions to keep out of his way meant nothing now that it was he who had banished her.

CHAPTER EIGHT

SHE hardly saw anything of Ryan for several days. When she got back from Port Gibson the atmosphere was tense and she learned that the executive producer had jetted in from England on a flying visit to check on production progress. Ryan was involved with him throughout that day and the next, and no one relaxed until he was on his way back home, apparently satisfied that money was being well spent.

Hanna had enjoyed her day with Aunt Rachael. Both Jay and Leigh were there and they all drove down to Natchez, which Hanna found quite captivating. The plantation houses were like something out of a dream, jewels at the heart of huge estates where water oaks were draped with Spanish moss. The restful beauty of a bygone age enchanted her, and she pictured Southern women in white crinolines languishing on the colonnaded galleries, and horse-drawn carriages arriving at the elegant front porticos. It was sad having to drag herself back to reality and she was tempted to linger, but Jay was worried about getting home in time for the dance.

'My friends'll love you,' he drawled, and she had to extricate herself from a possessive hug. 'I'll say they can look but not touch.'

But he had not counted on the stir a lovely young English girl would cause at his college and he found himself in the background once he had introduced her. There was great competition to dance with her and Hanna had never been so popular in her life. By the end of the evening she had hardly sat down or found time to eat, and fell exhausted into Jay's arms for a good old-fashioned last waltz.

'It's been wonderful,' she said. 'I don't know when I've enjoyed myself so much.'

'*I* haven't enjoyed myself at all,' Jay complained, 'until now. I'm the one who's taking you home, and boy, are they envious!'

Hanna laughed. 'You are a fool, Jay.'

His arms tightened about her and he kissed the top of her head. The long line of his body was against hers and he held her provocatively, but she felt no answering response, which made her sad. She had been trying for the past twenty-four hours to forget about Ryan Donalson, willing herself to feel for Jay the same excitement Ryan awakened in her, but it was useless. Only Ryan possessed the chemistry capable of creating fires in her, like touchpaper, and no way could she transfer it to Jay because she liked him better. There was nothing so mysterious as human nature.

Aunt Rachael looked at her questioningly the following morning, a worried little frown creasing her forehead. 'Something's bothering you, honey. You don't look so happy as you did the first day we saw you. You're kind of pensive. Aren't you contented to be with us?'

'Oh, Aunt Rachael, of course I am.' Hanna ran to hug her, putting her cheek against hers, and without warning she had to blink back idiotic tears. 'It's the other way round. I don't really want to go back to Vicksburg today.'

'Don't you like the work? Is it too much for you? I know you sat up late writing the night before last, I saw your light.'

'It's not the work,' said Hanna. 'I don't know what it is.'

The older woman touched her niece's hair fondly, the way her mother might have done, and tucked a curly strand behind her ear. 'I do,' she said. 'It's that big boss of yours. I saw him that first day, and Jay's mentioned him a few times. He's a whole hunk of man, and I guess you just don't know how to handle him. Am I right? You know, honey, your Uncle Jake was a bit like that. When he came along I wondered what had hit me.'

Hanna drew away. 'But I don't even like Ryan Donalson!'

'I didn't like your Uncle Jake, not at first.' Seeing Hanna's dismayed expression, her aunt gave a gentle laugh. 'Don't worry, honey, things always sort themselves out.'

'They already have,' said Hanna. 'In Ryan's books I'm just Jessica Franklin's secretary and he has to keep an eye on me for her sake.'

'Don't you be too sure!'

'And as regards female company while he's here Vicki Lander fills the bill, and I daresay he's picked out a string of other women for when he gets fed up with her. Honestly, I'm not the least bit bothered about him. I don't know why you think I should be.'

'If you say so,' said Aunt Rachael, her eyes twinkling. 'All I know is you've got someone on your mind, and you don't look back at Jay the way he looks at you, but I guess that was too much to hope for.'

'I'm sorry, Aunt Rachael. I hate hurting him.'

'He's still growing up, honey. He'll soon get over it. Even I can see he's far too immature to settle down.' Aunt Rachael got to her feet painfully and stood a moment to get her balance. 'Now give me a hand and we'll take a few steps round the garden before it gets too hot.'

She took Hanna's arm and they went outside, each step a small victory over the stiffness that attacked her after a night's rest, and Hanna marvelled at the way she stayed so cheerful. 'I think you're wonderful, Aunt Rachael,' she said. 'I love you, and I wish you didn't live so far away.'

Back in Vicksburg, she went straight to her room in the motel, much calmer than when she had left and determined not to let Ryan disturb her peace of mind any more. At lunch she met up with the other girls and was surprised when Vicki joined them until she heard about the arrival of the executive producer. With him around Ryan was kept fully occupied and everything else had to wait, even Vicki, presumably.

There was not a great deal for her to do. She typed out the scene she had written which was only short, but she had put a lot of thought into it and hoped Ryan would be pleased. The actual shooting of it would not take place until they were back in the studio at home.

Vicki was as friendly as ever, but no mention was made of Ryan and that was the way Hanna wanted it. She didn't think she could even talk about him without giving herself away, and for much the same reason she didn't go to places where he might be, because talking to him would be even worse. Just seeing him at a distance caused her heart to dance a peculiar jig, but she could cope with it and hoped it would soon wear off if no further fuel was added to the fire.

There was only one more big scene scheduled and then filming would be almost complete. She was getting bored without enough to do and it was Bill Hickly who took pity on her when he found her alone reading in the motel lounge.

'Hi, Hanna,' he said, 'I'm just going out to the Military Park before dinner to check a few things before tomorrow. Want to come with me?'

She liked Bill. He was losing his hair on top but had compensated for it by growing a neat brown beard, and his eyes shone beneath bushy brows.

'I'd like that,' said Hanna, and accompanied him happily.

Permission had been given for the Shirley House to be used for outside shots. Technicians had been busy all day preparing what they could and posts were ready for the arc lamps, positions marked out, and as they drove up the hill they saw the van that transported the generators. But Hanna had expected to see far more.

'What I don't understand,' she said, 'is how Ryan can possibly get the full effect. On old photos I've seen of the Shirley House during the Siege, the side of this hill was burrowed with caves and makeshift shelters where people hid from the shelling. I expected to see it all re-created.'

'It'll all be there,' Bill promised, with a smile, 'You'll see. In fact those scenes are already in the can.'

'They are?' She didn't know whether to believe him. 'But I never saw them being shot, and I'm sure I haven't missed anything.'

'They were done before we left England. It's all faked, Hanna. You remember we took shots of the house from a distance the other morning? Well, we incorporate those with battle scenes we filmed in a quarry back home and no one will ever know the difference, I assure you. I don't think the Department of the Interior would have appreciated us digging up their lovely park just so we could show it on television.'

Hanna laughed. 'No, I'm afraid they wouldn't.' She asked him a lot more questions and was quite fascinated to learn a lot more tricks of the trade. But besides being an interesting companion, he was also an amusing one and she enjoyed being with him immensely. It did her good to laugh.

And then out of the blue Bill gave her a piece of news that turned her ideas about Ryan upside down.

'You know, if it hadn't been for Vicki we would have been waiting around another week to do this scene.'

'What do you mean?'

'Didn't she tell you?' One furry eyebrow moved upwards like a caterpillar. 'About the crisis over the costumes? I thought you two were friends! I was having breakfast with Ryan before anyone was about when the post came and he had a letter confirming some dates from the theatrical costume people. He nearly hit the roof. Seems they'd slipped up somehwere, I don't know the details. Anyway, before you could say knife he'd phoned Vicki's room, and phoned the airport at Jackson to book a flight for her down to New Orleans. Then he drove her over to Jackson himself, and went back again in the evening to pick her up. I'll say this for him, he's got more energy than I've got.'

'Vicki went to New Orleans?' She stared at him incredulously.

'That's right. If she hadn't sorted things out personally we'd have been in a right mess.'

He went on talking about it, but Hanna wasn't listening. Vicki hadn't spent the night with Ryan, nor had they been together the next day as she had supposed. Her face burned with embarrassment at the way she had jumped to conclusions and she felt as though she had been caught out doing something really dreadful. She had maligned them, especially Ryan. There was a strange singing in her ears, a crescendo of heartbeats drumming a furious accompaniment, and she wanted to be alone with her thoughts.

She owed Ryan an apology, but how, and what was she going to say? She had the feeling he was avoiding her. During filming at the Shirley House next morning he only spoke to her once, and then so curtly it was as if he hardly noticed her. He was a stranger, barking instructions to his long-suffering team just as he had done on that day in London when she had first demanded to see him and then hoped it would be the one and only time. No different, yet now the thought of never seeing him again was too painful to contemplate. It was as though she were in love with him, but that was ridiculous. How could you possibly love someone and dislike him at the same time? It didn't make sense. She watched him all day delivering volleys of harsh words when things weren't done the way he wanted, and when the leading actress persistently stood in the wrong place he went over and moved her bodily to the right position, lashing her with criticism until it was a wonder she stayed. He was too arrogant by far, but that was the way he achieved the standard of perfection that had made him famous, and no one complained, at least not in his hearing.

And lying awake that night, still thinking about him, she knew there was another side to him that he kept hidden. She had glimpsed it once or twice, but feared she would never be one of the privileged few to whom it was shown.

She finally drifted into restless sleep and woke up at dawn. Her room was hot and oppressive and she couldn't stay in it any longer, so she hunted through her case until she found the swimsuit she had packed at the last minute, slipped it on and went down to the pool. The sun was not up, the air was blissfully cool, and there was no one around. She dived into the deep end and swam lazily from one end to the other and back, the exercise invigorating, the cold water making her skin tingle deliciously. She was a good swimmer, but her energy evaporated after a few laps and she let her body relax until she was floating on the surface, her mind now pleasantly at ease. The first shaft of sunlight glanced off a nearby roof and set the water gleaming. She closed her eyes.

She had drifted near to the end and the next thing she knew there was an almighty splash as someone jumped into the pool and grabbed her before she could regain control of her limbs. For a second she went under, then she struggled violently and yelled.

'Let me go. Let me go!' She was at the deep end and was spluttering as her hands grasped the tiled edge. When she opened her eyes it was Ryan who was there beside her and she was livid. 'What a *stupid* trick to play! You could have drowned me!'

'My God, Hanna, I thought you *had* drowned.' His face was pale and his hair crinkled close to his head, dripping wet. 'The sun was on the water and all I could see was a body floating on the top. It scared me, I can tell you.'

She was trembling, partly from shock and partly with cold now that she was out of the water. But more than anything she was shaken by the sudden nearness of Ryan.

He pulled himself up beside her, his body gleaming.

'You haven't driven me to suicide yet,' she said, covering her nervousness with a laugh. 'Though I bet there are a few people near to it after your temper yesterday!'

'Was I really that bad?' He looked genuinely surprised.

'I was just glad you were ignoring me.'

'Oh, Hanna!'

She had the upper hand and now she could cope, though for a minute she had been afraid he would see her agitation. Her heart was beating so hard it was almost visible through the thin material of her swimsuit and his eyes were on her, the expression in them disturbingly complicated. She pushed the wet hair away from her face, unable to look at him, and her nerves jerked her into hurried movement.

'I'll race you to the end,' she said, splashing into the water, and she headed for the opposite end with powerful strokes that worked the confusion temporarily out of her system. But he had caught up with her before she was halfway and grasped her ankle, making her stop and struggle. She cascaded the water over him furiously and he responded in kind until they were both laughing like children. To fend her off his long arms reached out in an attempt to grasp her shoulders, but as he did so his finger caught in the halter-neck strings at the back of her neck, pulling them undone, and the top of her swimsuit slipped. She gave a little scream and went to drag at it, but Ryan trapped both her wrists in one of his hands and drew her down beneath the surface, laughing still. All the air seemed to leave her lungs and she gasped for breath as she came up again, topless, angry and humiliated.

'Leave me alone, Ryan Donalson! I hate you!'

'It's all right, no one can see you. There aren't any windows facing the pool.'

'*You* can see me. Let me go!' She kicked out, but the water rendered it a useless exercise and she was still captive. He let her wrists go, but before she could slither away one arm was round her and he drew her back to where it was deeper.

'Now I'll turn my back while you tie your straps,' he said, his low voice husky.

She slipped downwards, away from him, but as she did so his hand travelled the length of her body, the sensuous movement an exquisite agony and every pulse throbbed. The water was just deep enough for her to stand and she secured the swimsuit with shaking fingers, not daring to look at him.

'I didn't mean that to happen. It was an accident, I assure you,' said Ryan.

'I don't believe it.'

He had climbed out of the pool and was vigorously towelling himself dry. In bathing trunks he seemed taller than ever and the sun catching his bronzed skin gave him the look of an athlete. She didn't have strength to move.

'Are you staying there all day?' he demanded.

'I'll come out when you've gone.' He must never know how she ached for him to touch her again.

He rubbed his hair and dried his face, purposely taking his time, and she saw a teasing smile turning up the corners of his mouth. Then he slung his towel over one shoulder and picked up hers before stretching out his hand to help her out.

'Come on, you'll get chilled.'

It was true she was shivering, and after a brief hesitation she accepted the strong hand, feeling his fingers curl round hers with tingling warmth. He rubbed her with the big bath towel, her bare back, her shoulders, her neck, so close to her she had only to turn and she would have been in his arms. It brought a choking sensation to her throat and when she could stand it no longer she snatched the towel and darted away.

'Thanks, I can finish,' she said.

She picked up her bath robe, slipped it on and tied it

round her waist, then tried to hurry away, but she had
to pass him and he stopped her.

'Hanna, don't go.'

He was not touching her, but their eyes met and held.
Both were breathing fast and she knew Ryan was
equally aware of the dangerous physical attraction that
encircled them like an ever-tightening band. Somehow
she had to break it.

'I must. I'm going to have a shower and get dressed.'

He ran his fingers through his damp hair to which the
curl was now returning, and frowned, as though trying
to restore normality. 'Look,' he said, 'would it help put
me back in everyone's good books if I let them have the
day off today, do you think? We're well up to schedule
and everybody would benefit from a break.'

'Are you asking me?'

'Yes. You said I was driving them suicidal.'

Hanna giggled, the easing of tension such a relief she
felt almost lightheaded. 'I didn't mean it. But now you've
suggested it I think it would be a very good idea.'

He began to stroll back towards the motel, Hanna
beside him. 'I'll arrange it then, on one condition.'

'And what's that?'

'That *you* don't go running off to spend the day with
your amorous cousin.'

She bristled. 'That's not the way to talk about Jay!
Anyway, what else can I do?'

'There's somewhere I'd like to take you,' he said. 'Will
you come with me?'

They were by the door and he faced her, his eyes
boring into her almost as though he was afraid she might
refuse, and she was filled with a new, overwhelming joy.
She was not going to question his reason for asking her.

'Of course I'll come.'

'Good.' He opened the door and held it so that she
had to duck her head under his arm to get inside. 'And
one more thing. Will you wear that green dress I first
saw you in?'

Back in her room she felt like singing out loud, but it was still early and people in the adjoining rooms would think she was mad. Instead she picked up her pillow and hugged it, dancing round until she was dizzy and fell across the bed in a whirl, forgetful of her wet swimsuit. Ryan wanted to spend the day with her. A whole day. Yesterday she would have refused in case he was playing her off against Vicki, but this morning was different now she knew it was not Vicki he wanted. She peeled off the swimsuit and stood a moment in front of the mirror. Her figure was good, her hair a bright colour. Ryan must like her a bit if he was willing to give up a day to take her out. She turned on the shower and stood under it, flexing her body with a new exhilaration before she dressed carefully, as he had asked, in the green shirtwaister that was Jessica's.

Oh, no! She was back where she had been at the start, before Vicki came on the scene. Supposing he had known all along that it was Jessica's dress? In the emotional turmoil of the last few hours she had forgotten about her, but there was no reason why Ryan should have done. So much had happened in Hanna's life since leaving London that it didn't seem possible it was less than two weeks. Two weeks was not long enough by any means to get over a broken love affair, especially when it was completely beyond recall, and she ought to have known it was only heartache that made him ask out the girl who reminded him of his lost love.

She dried her hair thoroughly, brushed it until it shone, then drew it up into a severe knot on top of her head. Over that she perched the white sunhat with the wide brim, and when she gave her appearance the final once-over she had to admit she looked good enough to take his mind off other things for a little while at least. And she was determined that nothing was going to spoil her day.

Ryan had arranged to meet her down at the car park in about an hour, giving him time to contact a few people and make sure there were no pressing commitments.

'We'll stop for breakfast at the first McDonald's we come to,' he said, 'then we can make an early start.'

She would have hated to keep him waiting, so she was there several minutes before he arrived, and when she saw him coming she gripped her hands together with trepidation, hardly able to believe she was going to have him to herself for the whole day. He wore his tight denim jeans, a white sports shirt, and carried a denim jacket. His eyes were hidden behind sunglasses, but when he came up to her she could tell she met with his approval by the tilt of his head and quick smile.

'Very nice,' he said warmly. But she knocked the hat as she got into the car and he reached over and removed it, putting it on the back seat. 'Keep that for the sun. I like to see your face so that I can tell when I've made you angry, then I can get ready to duck.'

Her cheeks coloured. 'You won't let me forget, will you?'

'Why should I?' He got in and started the engine before giving her another amused smile. 'You're the only woman who's ever attacked me, and I get the feeling you still haven't stopped fighting.'

She said nothing, but glanced at him sharply, wondering what his reaction would be if he knew the fight she had to put up was for self-preservation. It was a constant inner battle to try and get him out of her thoughts, and if she didn't keep her defences high that magnetism she had so far managed to resist would claim her and she would hate herself. She was not going to give him the slightest insight to her true feelings.

But she was willing to ease the situation for the next few hours. 'Perhaps we could call a short truce,' she said.

'A long truce would be even better. I'd hoped this lovely hot sun might thaw some of the icicles, but there's no sign of it yet.'

'I'm keeping in the shade. I'm told sunstroke is very unpleasant.'

Ryan's mouth tightened. The remark had been more pointed than she intended and she wished she could recall it, but it was too late.

He said: 'I get the message,' and drove swiftly out of town, while Hanna held her breath in case he decided to turn back. It was quite impossible to feel at ease with him.

But everything improved with breakfast. From the moment the girl behind the counter asked, 'How do you like your eggs?' and reeled off about half a dozen different variations from 'up and over' to 'sunny side up', the mood became lighter and they found they could laugh together. As long as they avoided each other's eyes and steered clear of undercurrents they could get along fine and began to find humour in the simplest things which would have seemed ridiculous to anyone else.

In the car again she even dared to ask where they were going. 'This is the road to Port Gibson, and I've been to Natchez.'

'Impatient Miss Ballantyne,' he chided. 'Have you ever been to Windsor Castle?'

'Now you're teasing me!'

'On the contrary, that's where I'm taking you. It's a fascinating place, but I doubt if you'll find any resemblance to the one at home.'

'Who lives there?'

'No one,' said Ryan, and when she went on asking questions all he would answer was, 'Wait and see. I hope you won't be disappointed. Somehow I'm sure you'll feel the way I do about it.'

He turned off at Port Gibson and for a while they fell into a companionable silence. Traffic was almost nil and the road seemed narrow now she had become used to the wide, hectic freeways. There was even a bend or two, and as they drove deeper into the country the scenery changed dramatically. A sea of Black-eyed

Susans decked the roadside like little yellow hats with tall black crowns, but what Hanna loved most were the huge magnolia trees in fields and gardens, waxen blooms still glowing among the dark green leathery leaves although it was getting late in the season. Whenever she saw them from now on she would remember this day with Ryan.

'I never imagined magnolias growing wild like this,' she sighed. 'They're so beautiful.'

'Mississippi used to be called the Magnolia State,' he said. 'I think it was a pity to change it.'

Gradually the sassafras and sweet gum trees became a thick forest and when the sun went in it was quite eerie. A creeper which Ryan said someone had once brought from the Orient seemed to cover everything with its huge leaves and it was more like being in a jungle. And the road went on for ever.

A flutter of apprehension made Hanna sit forward, hoping for open ground again at every turn, and Ryan smiled as he looked at her. But at last the trees thinned out and the sun reappeared, and there on the left was Windsor Castle.

It was an extraordinary sight, a ruin miles from anywhere with just twenty-two Corinthian columns pointing skywards. In its day it must have been palatial, and Hanna gazed in wonder at all that was left.

'It's beautiful!' she gasped.

'Or ugly,' Ryan suggested. He turned off the road on to a rough, bumpy track and drove right up to the ruins.

'No, it's not ugly,' she said, standing by the stark columns and looking up. 'I think it's unbearably sad. I've never seen anything like it.' Tears welled up in her eyes and she turned away, surprised to see the Mississippi River shining in the distance.

'That's how I feel about it, too. I came here once before, alone. I just sat here for hours. Something about the place made me stay, like tentacles drawing me back into the past. I can't really explain.'

'What happened to it?' asked Hanna.

'There was a fire, about 1890 or thereabouts. They say Mark Twain stayed here. He could look out across the river from the windows.'

By the fence there was a bush of red roses and he picked a bud, handing it to her without another word. She took it and held it to her nose, sniffing the faint perfume, then tucked it in the brim of her hat, hoping it wouldn't wilt too much because she was going to press it for a keepsake. How Ryan would laugh if he knew!

He sank down on the grass with a sigh of contentment, and after a moment she sat beside him. It was so quiet. The only sound was the skittering of tree frogs. Ryan had closed his eyes. It was the first time she had seen him relaxed and she was able to look at him without detection, mentally tracing every line of his face so that she would always remember. And as she looked at him, committing to memory each mark on his skin, the way his hair grew, the set of his ears, the shape of his nose, the distinctive, arrogant slant of his eyebrows and forehead, the firm mouth and craggy jaw, there was suddenly a great happiness radiating through her, bringing with it the certainty instead of suspicion that this was love. She loved him. All this time it was love that had flooded her heart and spilled over into senseless belligerence because she hadn't understood. Nor would she ever express it. Ryan was not for her, she knew that. She was not clever or talented like Jessica, or self-confident and chic like Vicki. He was a brilliant man, way beyond her, and he was merely amusing himself by taking her out while there was no one else who took his fancy.

As he sensed her scrutiny his drowsy lids lifted before she was aware of it and she was afraid he might have seen the adoration she was too slow to hide. She turned her head. The hot sun was blinding and the sound of the tree frogs was synonymous with the heat. He propped himself up on one elbow and reached up to draw the pins out of her hair one by one until it spilled in fierce glory round her shoulders. She didn't stop him. The merest touch of his fingers on her hair was ecstasy.

'It doesn't suit you up like that,' he said. 'You look like a schoolmarm. Sometimes you even act like one, but there's another side of you, isn't there . . . reserved perhaps for Jay Caldwell.'

She wanted to deny it, tell him there was absolutely nothing between her and Jay and never would be, but she was too choked to speak, and as Ryan couldn't see her face he took her silence to mean agreement. Her legs were doubled under her and she moved, intending to get up, but he anticipated it and caught her wrist, forcing her to stay, and with the other hand he jerked her head round.

'Okay, so he's the important one.' His voice was sharp. 'But you're with me today, so we'll forget about him.'

The grip on her arm was like a vice, and there was nothing she could do to prevent his mouth coming down on hers with brutal force. She twisted round, intent on pushing him away, but it only made it easier for him to hold her and she fell back on to the ground. The coarse grass cut against her cheeks as she tossed her head from side to side, but the pressure of his lips increased and finally she had no resistance. Kissing him was like tasting potent wine and craving for more until intoxication was so sweet all else was blotted out. Her arms came up round his neck, her fingers twined in the thick brown hair, touching it for the first time, revelling in the primeval excitement of physical contact, and her fingers clenched, pulling his hair until pain transmitted itself and he lifted his head. For a second he looked down at her, then groaned and buried his face against her neck, kissing her throat, and the closeness of his body beside hers sent flames roaring through her.

She opened her eyes when there was a shrill bird cry

from one of the nearby trees, and thinking it was someone coming she sprang away from his arms.

'Please, Ryan, please, don't!' she cried, and got hurriedly to her feet, trembling so much she swayed and almost fell.

Ryan stared at her, his eyes bright and feverish. 'Now I know,' he murmured, the words measured and full of meaning. Know what? Was he really aware how close she had been to letting that first experience of overwhelming temptation take over completely. 'If you respond to cousin Jay like that no wonder he's infatuated!'

He lay back and rolled over on to his stomach, his face hidden in the grass. Still trying to regain her breath, she hesitated, the longing to kneel down and caress him so strong she had to clench her hands. Then she turned away abruptly and started walking on shaky legs, wishing the overgrown ruins afforded a little shade so that she could cool down. She felt the pull of them. There had been people here who knew what she was going through and sympathised. Passions had run deep, drama and tragedy had happened on this spot when those huge, sad columns had supported a roof and walls and galleries. She was not alone. Maybe it was the first time anything like this had happened to Hanna Ballantyne, but her emotions were as old as time and she would recover.

He didn't follow her. She wandered alone, deep in thought, careless of the rough turf scratching her feet, and she didn't realise until it was too late that the little mound of soil deceptively like the rest was an anthill. Within seconds of treading on it her foot was covered in big black ants that stung, and her screams carried back to Ryan. By the time he reached her she had frantically dislodged most of them, but already red blotches were appearing on her skin and the colour had drained from her face.

'They're fire ants,' Ryan told her. Her eyes were wide

with fear. 'You'll have some infected spots by tomorrow and they'll itch like fury, but they won't hurt you. Look, there's a puddle over there. We'll bathe your foot.'

He picked her up and carried her down an incline to where muddy water was lying in a shallow pool, undid her sandal and put her foot in the water. Luckily the blotches began to fade when he rubbed them with some leaves and there were only three or four stings.

'It was awful,' she said unsteadily. 'I was terrified!'

'Poor Hanna! That's two shocks you've given me today. What are you trying to do to me?' He stood up and smiled at her gently. 'Come on, I'll carry you back to the car.'

'I can walk,' she protested.

'And let you put your foot in it a third time! I'm not risking it.'

He scooped her up in his arms and strode down the path as though she was weightless. She laughed, clutching his shoulder, and the hard muscles moved under her touch. When he set her down her arms stayed round his neck and he held her tenderly, cradling her head against his chest where she could hear the wild beating of his heart, and she longed to stay there indefinitely. He kissed the top of her head, catching a strand of hair round his finger, and as she looked up he kissed her mouth. It was not like before. This time there was gentleness in the play of his lips upon hers and she melted against him, limp with happiness.

'Oh, Hanna,' he murmured, stroking her face. 'I've kept out of your way the last couple of days. I should have done the same today.'

But why? her heart cried out. She had never been so deliriously happy in all her life. If he was feeling anything like the same then why did the kissing have to stop? She had only to recognise the dangerous, pulsating excitement through her body to know the answer. A new quietness descended on them as they got in the car, and common sense gradually returned. She ought to be glad Ryan was not prepared to embark on a casual affair. Had such a thing happened it could only last until they got back to England and they would be parted by the differences in their background and personalities. She would never be strong enough to hold him. Anyway, she had been brought up to believe in marriage and her parents would be bitterly disappointed if she settled for anything less, and it would never be worth all the heartbreak. And Ryan already knew the meaning of that.

As the day wore on she began to scoff at herself for reading too much into a few kisses. Ryan reverted to his normal self, sometimes involving her in deep discussion, sometimes making a remark that aggravated and when she replied in kind there was amusement in the quirk of his eyebrow, which was even more annoying. But on the whole she was full of optimism, and was sorry when they got back to the motel late in the afternoon.

'Thank you,' she said, before getting out of the car. 'It's been the loveliest day.'

'I'm glad.' He leaned forward, as if to kiss her again, and her heart lurched.

'Ryan . . .'

'Yes?'

But she shook her head and opened the car door quickly, otherwise she would have blurted out how much she loved him and that would have been fatal. They went into the motel together, and just before entering the lounge he caught hold of her hand.

'Thank you, too,' he said softly, and pushed open the door.

There were several people having drinks before dinner and he dropped her hand, but not before the little scene had been witnessed. Hanna looked across the room and her limbs turned to ice, for there, standing alone, was the last person in the world she had expected to see.

It was Jessica.

CHAPTER NINE

AFTER the initial shock of seeing her, Hanna's chief reaction was pleasure at the arrival of a familiar face, and she prepared to go and meet her without considering the effect *she* would have on Jessica. She hurried towards her, a smile of welcome already on her lips.

'Jessica, what a wonderful surprise . . .'

But Jessica brushed her aside as though she was a stranger and flung herself at Ryan. Her hands fastened round his neck and she was sobbing in his arms.

'Oh, Ryan, I can't tell you how I've longed to see you,' she cried. 'I've been quite desperate!'

People in the lounge returned to their drinks and interrupted conversations, pretending not to notice, and all Hanna could do was stand by helplessly and watch.

'You're supposed to be on honeymoon in Italy,' said Ryan, his brows drawn together in perplexity. 'Where's Alistair? Is he with you?'

Jessica's tears flowed. 'Darling, darling Ryan, it was the biggest mistake I ever made. How could you let me make such a terrible mistake?'

He put a finger on her lips, trying to draw her away from inquisitive eyes and ears, but she would not be moved. Her beautiful black hair was cut short and her big brown eyes were full of childlike accusation. How could *she* be so unreasonable?

'When did you ever ask advice before doing anything?' Ryan countered, talking to her as if she was a wayward child. He smiled down at her, held her protectively. Hanna saw the change in him and the ache in her heart was worse than anything she could have imagined.

'You promised to bring me back here for the location

work,' Jessica said. 'It was where we first had the idea for *Forty-seven Days*. You *promised* me, Ryan—then waited until I was out of the way. I wouldn't have believed it of you!'

Feeling she must say something, Hanna interposed: 'I can explain, Jessica . . .'

'Why do you think I phoned you that morning?' said Ryan. 'We needed you.'

'We? What do you mean, we?' She was getting almost hysterical and it was so embarrassing Hanna wanted to hide. The next volley was even worse. 'As soon as my back was turned you flew off with that traitorous little bitch I employed as a secretary. I won't let her get away with it!'

She spoke as though Hanna wasn't there, and above her head Hanna's eyes met Ryan's, imploring him to do something about it. She would have expected his temper to flare, but there was little sign of emotion in his expression. His control was superb. But then, of course, he loved Jessica. To have her appear like this, regretting her marriage and throwing herself at him, was wonderful for his over-inflated ego. Everyone could see what a fantastic, irresistible creature he was.

'It's all right, Jess,' he said, his quiet voice soothing her. 'We'll get it all sorted out.'

Hanna could have hit him. It didn't matter to him that she had been publicly insulted, falsely accused and made to look like a fool, as long as Jessica was consoled! Well, she wasn't going to stay there and be laughed at by everyone within earshot!

'Excuse me,' she said, razor-sharp.

She marched from the lounge out into the foyer, intent on escaping to her room so that she could give vent to her feelings, but on the way she collided headlong with Jay. He steadied her, laughing, not realising it was turmoil that caused her haste.

'Hey, what's gotten into you?' he challenged.

The stress of the day was catching up with her and

when Jay held her at arm's length and looked questioningly into her eyes it was difficult to hold back tears.
She needed to talk to someone, Aunt Rachael preferably,
but Jay was the next best thing, and he couldn't have
come at a better time. Somehow she produced an over-
bright smile.

'Why nothing. I was just going to change in case you
came over this evening.'

'Liar,' he said, in the kindest way. 'I guess I don't
have to look farther than a certain TV director to know
who's been upsetting you. If I could get my hands on
that guy . . .'

'Jay, please!' Her composure was finely balanced and
it only needed a word more of sympathy to tilt her into
an attack of self-pity, a state she had no time for in
others and would despise even more in herself.

'Okay. How about finding a quiet place for a meal?'

'I'd like that. If you don't mind waiting I really must
tidy myself up, but I'll be as quick as I can.'

'For you I'd wait for ever,' he said gallantly.

She got to her room and leaned back against the door,
fists clenched, and for a moment she froze into a kind
of shocked immobility. Ryan had his Jessica back—the
woman he loved. And from the way he had ignored her
silent plea just now it was obvious he had no further use
for Hanna Ballantyne. With Jessica once more available
nothing else mattered. Nothing, and no one. She
squared her shoulders and took a deep breath. The first
thing to do was try to cancel out the discovery she had
made this morning. It ought to be easy enough. She
must keep reminding herself that Ryan was a pompous,
uncharitable egotist who used people to get what he
wanted and then discarded them, and was quite impossible to love. She had known from the first that he
was treacherous and not to be trusted at any cost.

There were only two days left of their stay in
Vicksburg and she supposed she would have to stick
them out. Perhaps he wouldn't even notice if she packed

her bags and went over to Aunt Rachael's. But no. She drew herself up and the unshed tears that kept threatening were replaced by the glitter of temper. Her fighting spirit was roused. Why should she go skulking off as if she had done something wrong? It was all Ryan's doing that she was here and she had every right to stay and finish the job she had started.

Her mind clearer, she showered and changed into another dress, and knotted her hair up out of the way. She was not going to give Ryan Donalson another thought, and she would shelve the sticky problem of Jessica until tomorrow when she would have had time to gather fresh courage to face the fireworks. Tonight she would be nice to Jay.

He looked relieved to see her smiling more naturally when she joined him about twenty minutes later and linked his arm through hers as they went out to the car. 'Your boss just left with a neat little brunette clinging to him,' he said.

'Correction,' said Hanna. 'The brunette is, or was, my boss, not Ryan Donalson.'

'I don't get it.'

'That was Jessica Franklin, just flown over from England, minus her husband.'

'Halle—lujah!'

'And by tomorrow I'll probably be out of a job.' She glanced at him with a grin. 'I thought about crying on your shoulder just now, but I've changed my mind. They're not worth bothering about, and I really don't care.'

'That's the spirit,' said Jay, but he could see the underlying strain and attributed it entirely to Jessica, knowing nothing of the deeper emotional involvement that complicated Hanna's problems. He only knew it was necessary to cheer her up, and promptly set out to amuse her.

The quiet meal was scrapped in favour of a pizza parlor—no chance there to brood. After that he took her to a drive-in movie and plied her with Coke and hamburgers until she protested she couldn't possibly eat another thing and her main worry changed to the amount of weight she would put on.

'Nonsense,' said Jay. 'You'll always have that perfect figure.'

The movie was over, but they were still sitting in the car waiting to get out of the grounds. 'Not if I lived here all the time I wouldn't,' she laughed.

'Want to bet?'

'I'm not likely to find out anyway.'

He paused thoughtfully. The film had been very funny and they had laughed a lot, which was the kind of tonic he had planned for her, but in the midst of the fun it was clear that he, too, had something on his mind.

'Hanna,' he said slowly, 'Momma settled out here in Mississippi and now she wouldn't live anywhere else. Do you think you could, too?'

She had enjoyed the evening more than she would have thought possible, and she had to avoid seriousness creeping in to spoil it. So she answered lightly, 'I hope that's a hypothetical question.'

'Not necessarily. You said you might be out of a job. Couldn't you apply for a work permit and get a job here? You could come and live with us.'

'And leave my parents? They'd be very upset.'

'If you married an American, like Momma did, you'd have to leave them,' he persisted.

'But I'm not going to do that.' Her tone was firm.

Jay took hold of both her hands in his. 'Why not, Hanna? I want to marry you, and I'll take great care of you. Right now I want to go and shake that woman for making you so upset.'

'Oh, Jay!' His boyish eyes were full of concern. And love. She could see sincerity in every line of his face, feel it in the pressure of his fingers. She couldn't hurt him by refusing outright, even if she wanted to, and she was no longer sure about that. After the tumult of the last

few hours she had begun to think love at fever pitch
was too exhausting to be endured and there was much
to be said for an undemanding affection that would
grow slowly into a lasting love over the years. But it
had to be undemanding on both sides and she couldn't
imagine Jay agreeing to a long engagement, even though
he had declared he would wait for ever. 'I really don't
think we've known each other long enough . . .'

'I knew I wanted to marry you as soon as I saw you.'

And Ryan has got Jessica. The repetitive words
chanted through her mind like a jingle, over and over,
refusing to go. No hope now of winning him herself, if
that had been her subconscious ambition. She shivered.
What hope had she ever had anyway. It was a pity
Jessica hadn't arrived yesterday. Perhaps it would have
saved all this heart-searching, because yesterday she had
still been fairly resistant to Ryan Donalson's magnetism.

Mistaking her silence for hopeful hesitation, Jay
leaned forward and kissed her, his lips gentle as if he
was afraid of scaring her, and not attempting to stir up
the sort of emotion Ryan induced. She wanted to turn
her head away because the reminder of this morning's
kisses was too acute, but mindful of her resolution she
used all her will power to concentrate only on Jay. At
least when she did draw away he had no idea that there
had been any comparison to make.

'Promise me you'll think about it, Hanna,' he said.

She smoothed a lock of silky fair hair away from his
forehead. 'I promise.'

It was late when she returned to the motel and she
fell into bed, too tired to worry any more about the
complications suddenly disrupting her previously uncomplicated life. In the morning sparks might fly, but
things were never so frightening in daylight.

There was a buzz around the dining room next morning, stories of Jessica's unexpected arrival gathering
momentum until they became a drama of gossip column

proportions. As neither she nor Ryan appeared at breakfast to give the lie to any of it, it was Hanna who came in to a barrage of questions. The girls had accepted her now as one of themselves and couldn't wait to hear any scandal she might know about her script-writer boss who had deserted her husband after less than a fortnight and flown half across the world into the arms of her former lover. It was a better tale than anything to be seen on television.

'I should have grabbed him while he was free,' wailed Vicki, and Hanna was uncomfortably reminded of the wrong conclusion she had jumped to earlier in the week. 'I should have made him come to New Orleans that day and seduced him.'

'You mean to say he didn't suggest it himself,' teased one of the girls. 'You must be slipping, Vicki.'

'You could tell he had someone else on his mind.'

'He frightens me to death,' said another girl. 'What's her husband like?'

Hanna described Alistair Kerby as best she could after the one brief meeting, and there was simply nothing else she could tell them. It had been the whirlwind romance to end all whirlwind romances.

'So what will you do now?' Vicki asked her.

Hanna felt rather than saw Ryan approach their table. She had glimpsed him coming in through the main door, his hair damp from his usual morning swim, and she clasped her hands in her lap so that no one could see she was trembling. It made her so cross. Why couldn't she just stop reacting to him in this ridiculous way? At Vicki's question she lifted her chin and paused long enough for him to come within hearing distance.

'I'm thinking about marrying my cousin Jay Caldwell,' she said.

There was a clamour of comment, but that was all she would say, and it had been purely for Ryan's benefit. She merely smiled as if it were a secret she was keeping.

And her heart was thudding louder in her ears than the voices round her. She could only think, 'That'll show him!'

Ryan stood between her and Vicki, a hand on each of their shoulders, but it was to Hanna he spoke. 'I'd like a word with you when you've finished breakfast.'

'I've finished now,' she said, and stood up. He gave her one of his special smiles. Damn him!

'It's the final day of filming,' he went on, when they were a little way apart from the others. 'It's the re-take of the Balfour House shots, as you know, but I think it might be better if you give it a miss. I'm sure you understand.'

'Oh, yes,' she answered, 'I understand perfectly. But as I was asked to come out here and do a job, I prefer to see it through to the end. If Jessica wants me to hand back the work I'll be happy to discuss it with her, but if she wants to go on pretending I'm not here perhaps you'll be good enough to explain as you seem to be able to deal with her.'

'Hanna ...' His voice was coaxing, trying to recall her when she had marched defiantly away with her head held high. Had she listened she would have detected real concern, and would have saved herself a showdown, but pride was all-important and she would not be cast off unfairly.

She was waiting in the foyer for Bill to pick her up and take her in his car over to the location site when the confrontation with Jessica happened. The weather was heavy and overcast. A downpour in the morning had delayed filming, making everyone irritable at the prospect of finishing late on the last day, and it was now after lunch. Ryan issued abrupt orders, his mood obviously brittle, and looks were exchanged in silent agreement that it would be unwise to cross him. Hanna was surprised. She thought he ought to be happy, but there was no pleasing him, and she was glad when he said he had urgent phone calls to make and would meet them down there later.

He had only been gone a few minutes when Jessica appeared. She made straight for Hanna.

'I don't know how you've got the nerve to stand there with my files and scripts in your hand,' she snapped, not bothering to lower her voice. 'You're so brazen it's unbelievable!'

Hanna's face coloured at the unwarranted attack in front of a small crowd, but she was not daunted. 'I explained everything in the letter I left for you. Surely you read it when you got to the house?'

'Of course, and I didn't believe a word of it. Can you imagine the shock I had, arriving back to find you'd ransacked my house, taken half my things, including my job and the only man I've ever loved, and beaten a retreat across the Atlantic! What with that coming on top of everything else, I almost had a nervous breakdown. You're a worthless little troublemaker, and a thief into the bargain!'

'Jessica, what a terrible thing to say! I demand an apology.' Hanna could hardly believe this was the same person as the one she had known in London, her rather zany, happy-go-lucky boss who had made work a pleasure.

'You don't like home truths, do you, Hanna?' sneered Jessica.

'None of that is the truth, and you know it!'

The foyer had emptied quickly. Hurried glances of sympathy were directed at Hanna, but no one wanted to get involved and the two girls were soon alone, much to Hanna's relief. She couldn't escape.

But Jessica was oblivious to everyone. 'When you came in yesterday you were wearing my dress. You can't deny it. My photo of Ryan is missing. No doubt that's somewhere in your luggage. Did you think I wouldn't miss things? My notes are right there in that folder, which I should like to have, if you please.'

She held out her hand, but Hanna ignored it and took a tighter grip on the zip-topped leather folder under her arm.

'The photograph is in a drawer in your bedroom,' Hanna told her. 'I put it there because I didn't think your husband would like to see a picture of your ex-lover by the bed. The dress I'm sorry about, but I can explain . . .'

'You took it because you thought wearing my clothes was a way of getting Ryan. Well, you'll never have him! He loves me.'

'Yes,' said Hanna, 'he does. Though I can't think why after the disgraceful way you've treated him. Running off like that and getting married was the most stupid thing I've ever heard of. If you love Ryan why on earth did you do it?'

'It's none of your business, but if you must know, Ryan will never get married. He's told me so often enough. He likes his freedom too much, but Alistair was willing to give up everything for me.'

'And even that wasn't enough, it seems.'

They were shouting at each other, though Hanna was trying hard to show some restraint. A slanging match was the last thing she had wanted.

'I will *not* discuss my marriage with you,' Jessica snapped. 'But your job is another matter. Ryan told me how you practically blackmailed him into bringing you along so that you could see your beastly relations on the cheap . . .'

'It's a lie! I'm certain he never said any such thing.'

'You've altered my scripts without my permission, and even had the audacity to write another scene and insist that Ryan includes it. For your information, it's terrible, and we've had a good laugh over it. Ryan is going to tear it up. And as from now you're out of a job, because you needn't think *I'm* going to pay you anything, and I'll make sure you don't get included on the Beauman Studios payroll.'

Hanna couldn't stand any more of the vitriolic outbursts. She pushed the leather folder into Jessica's arms with such force she almost overbalanced, and stalked away from her with as much dignity as she could muster.

Having fled from Jessica, instinct propelled her towards the privacy of her own room where she could lick her wounds and try to recover from the humiliation and hurt she had suffered, but before she was halfway up the stairs anger was uppermost, directed not at the woman whose vindictiveness had cut like a whiplash, but at Ryan Donalson who seemed to have misled her maliciously on all counts. He had promised to make everything right with Jessica as soon as he saw her, but not only had he gone back on his word, he had ridiculed her into the bargain and made up outright lies. Part of her denied that he was capable of such wickedness, but the seeds of doubt were firmly planted. He was a walking success story, and he probably hadn't got where he was without treading on a few people along the way. People were expendable. And he would need to impress Jessica in order to regain her confidence, so what did it matter if a mere secretary's character was blackened? Well, it did matter very much, and she was sure as hell going to put up a fight.

Her footsteps slowed and she remembered he was making phone calls and would be in his room. She would go up there now and challenge him. He had a lot of explaining to do and if necessary she would force him to repeat in front of Jessica what he had originally said in order to get her to come unwillingly to the States. Surely he had a spark of decency somewhere? She would tell him exactly what she thought of him, demand an explanation and an apology, and then she never wanted to see him again. Never!

She passed her own door and went farther along to Ryan's. It was ajar. She spoke his name sharply and went in before her courage dwindled. Looked around. The room was empty and there was not a sign of him anywhere, but a clipboard and several of his books and papers were on the table, spread out as if he was coming back to them. And beside them were his keys. Hanna glanced at everything briefly and was about to leave, almost crying with frustration, when her eyes returned involuntarily to the keys. More than anything she wanted to see Aunt Rachael. Her aunt was the only one she could fly to and know she would be believed, and the longing for a pair of motherly arms to give comfort had reached the desperate stage. Her hand reached out and before she had time to consider the stupidity of it, the keys were in her handbag. Then without anyone seeing her she slipped back down the stairs and out into the car park.

The Buick was there in its usual place. If she had been in a rational state of mind nothing would have induced her to get in it, let alone start it, but desperation crushed any fear she might have had of handling such a large car and coping with the unfamiliar left-hand drive. Her father had always had a large car and had taught her to drive in it as soon as she was old enough, so the size was not really so important, but she had to spend several precious minutes getting the feel of it before she dared to take it out on the road. And then she was away.

She had travelled the road to Port Gibson enough times now to be fairly used to it, and as she drove along at the regulation fifty-five miles an hour she felt the tension begin to ease. It was good to be behind a wheel. She had always enjoyed driving and missed her own little car when she went to work in London and decided against keeping it. The feel of the Buick was exhilarating, and the fact that she had taken it without permission was neither here nor there. What did she care if Ryan Donalson set the police on her trail? Aunt Rachael would make everything right. Nevertheless, when a police car passed her going the other way her heart did a frightened lurch, and she had a horrible dread of hearing a siren coming up behind her for the next few miles. If he reported it stolen she would be driving a wanted car. But the farther she got from Vicksburg the easier it was to convince herself he wouldn't even miss it before she got back, and if he did she hoped he would realise it was she who had inconvenienced him and contain his fury until they came face to face.

She drew up outside her aunt's house and sank back into the seat a moment, feeling like a homing pigeon. Whatever would she have done without Aunt Rachael to turn to? It was a quiet road and there was no one about as she walked up to the front door and rang the bell. With fresh despair she saw there were letters still in the mail box, and no one came.

'Mizz Rachael ain't here today. Don't you know, it's her treatment day at the hospital.' A large woman of about forty had appeared in the next-door garden wearing shorts that emphasised her ample proportions and a headscarf over jumbo-sized rollers.

'No, I didn't know,' said Hanna. 'Isn't there anybody in?'

'I guess not, honey. Hey, you'll be her niece from England, the one with the fantastic job in television. I'm right glad to meet you. Say, why don't you come on over and have a Coke or some coffee and you can tell me all about that fabulous man Mizz Rachael says you work for. Do you know, I've never met anyone before who worked in television . . .'

'It's very kind of you,' Hanna interrupted, trying to edge away. 'Another time I'd like to come and have a talk, but I'm in an awful rush right now. Forgive me.'

She ran back down the path and into the car before the woman could see there were tears streaming down her cheeks. She drove a little way, but her vision was too blurred for safety and she pulled in again a couple of blocks away, crossed her arms over the steering wheel and buried her head in them as she gave way to choking sobs. She hardly ever cried, but she had counted on

Aunt Rachael's sympathy, and finding she was not there was yet another blow.

After a few minutes she felt better and opened her eyes. She could smell the leather covering on the wheel and as she lifted her head her hands slowly explored the rim. Yesterday Ryan's hands had guided the car, touched where her hands were touching now.

She couldn't go back to the motel. She was too over-wrought to face anyone yet, but she couldn't stay by the roadside either, blocking someone's drive indefinitely. She glanced round. On the opposite corner there was a signpost showing the direction of Windsor Castle. She closed her eyes tight, squeezing out the imprint of the sign, refusing to see it. But when she opened her eyes again a new calmness enveloped her. Yesterday she had been happy.

She followed the sign automatically at an easy pace, remembering the trees and flowers she had passed, nodding to the Black-eyed Susans, smiling at the magnolias and dogwood trees. This was better than talking to anyone. An hour or two alone in the place where memories were sweet and quietness lulled the mind like old wine would do her more good than tearing off back to chaotic civilisation.

But she had forgotten the long stretch of creeper-covered forest that had even made her shiver when Ryan was beside her. It was darker and more mysterious than before, lonely, eerie and damp. She couldn't see the sky, but the first spots of rain on the windscreen were as big as ten-pence pieces, and were the ominous forerunners of a deluge. She kept on going. There were no places to turn and she guessed she would be out of the trees sooner this way than if she turned back. The windscreen wipers couldn't cope with the water and she had to peer through rain-lashed windows that were like frosted glass. And the beating of the rain on the car roof was deafening—so deafening that she didn't hear the first clap of thunder.

When she left the comparative shelter of the trees she met the full impact of the storm. She had never seen such a terrible sky in her life, and as the inky blackness hanging above the Mississippi was torn apart by fork lightning she was so terrified she lost control of the car and swerved off the road, bumping, jolting, careering through rough earth until mud checked the speed. Finally it came to a stop in a clump of spiky bushes.

The last thing she remembered seeing was the stark columns of Windsor Castle etched into a brilliant white flash of sheet lightning, and her screams were lost in the thunderclap that followed immediately after it.

CHAPTER TEN

WHEN she opened her eyes it was still raining. She was lying across the front seat with her arms over her head, and she was dreaming Ryan called her name. The voice was insistent. When she didn't answer, it became angry.

'For God's sake, Hanna, what do you think you're doing out here alone, miles from anywhere? And what the hell do you mean by crashing my car into a bush? If you've damaged it the hire firm won't let me off lightly, and I've a damn good mind to send the bill to you!'

The car door was open and rain splashed in on her face. She moved slowly, but her limbs were unwilling to respond and all she did was turn on to her back. And that was when she discovered it was not the rain but Ryan's wet hair that dripped on her as he leaned over, trying to rouse her.

'Your language is disgraceful, Mr Donalson,' she said, her own voice sounding as if it didn't belong to her. She didn't know what he was doing there, but he was behaving true to form and the obstinate streak that would not allow his arrogance to go unchallenged gave her sufficient strength to try and push him away. Then she sat up.

He moved back, making room for her. 'Oh, Hanna, you gave me the fright of my life,' he said, in a totally different tone. He gathered her into his arms, holding her against him for several seconds. His hands caressed the back of her neck and lifted her hair, crushing it like silk in his strong fingers. 'Darling, I'm so sorry I shouted, but it was the only way I could be sure of getting through to you.'

Still thinking she was dreaming Hanna nestled against his chest. His shirt was wet, open almost to the waist

156

and clinging to him. Wiry hair was rough to her cheek
and she rubbed against it, her eyes closed. He had called
her darling. That proved nothing was real. Only in
dreams did such wonderful things happen. His face
touched the top of her head and he groaned, then his
hands slid down to her shoulders and he shook her until
she cried out.

'I ought to beat the living daylights out of you. What
a stupid, crazy, mindless thing to do!' he muttered, his
eyes blazing. 'What on earth possessed you to steal my
keys and take off in a car you've never handled before?
On roads like this it's a wonder you survived at all!'

This was no dream. He was quivering with anger.
Rain hammered on the car roof with renewed ferocity
and she struggled to free herself from his furious grasp.

'What would it matter if I hadn't survived? It's a pity
you found me.'

'Don't talk utter rubbish!'

'I'm saying that no way could I stay in the motel any
longer being humiliated and slandered. I ought to have
driven the other way to the airport and got on the first
flight home!'

'And I'm saying that you're still my responsibility and
you'll stay here until *I* decide when you go home!'

It was hot in the car, but it was nothing compared
with the heat of their tempers as they shouted at each
other.

'Not any longer,' said Hanna, seething. 'Thanks to
you Jessica has fired me, so I'm free to go where I like.'

'Not in my car you're not!'

'Then drive me back to Port Gibson and I'll go to my
aunt's. At least there's someone there who cares about
me.'

His mouth was set in a firm line, his broad shoulders
squared and forbidding, and there was not an ounce of
compassion in him.

'I got the message first thing,' he said, his eyes meeting
hers with increased hostility. 'But now is not the time to

discuss your personal affairs, or what went on between you and Jessica.'

Hanna gasped with anger. 'That's right, evade the issue! Make out you had nothing to do with the things Jessica said. If it makes it easier for you to go back on your word and side with her, then good luck! See if I care!'

Ryan drew a long breath and let it out slowly, and the mocking tone gradually returned to his voice, as if he was dealing with a wayward child.

'Hanna, I'm sorry about the trouble with Jessica. It's obviously upset you very much, but you ought to know by now how vindictive she can be—and how unpredictable. But right this minute we've got more important things to think about. This rain has been going on for a couple of hours or more. The road is flooding fast.'

She stared at him, readjusting her thoughts with difficulty. Then she looked out of the window. The road was several yards away to their right and she saw another car drawn in to the side, the one Ryan had used to follow her. Water was all around them like a lake, the coarse grass only showing through where there were mounds of earth, and though the road was visible it was completely awash. And still the rain poured down.

'What are we going to do?' she asked anxiously.

'First we've got to see what damage you've done to the car and see if it's possible to get it back on firm ground. Move over and let me try it.'

'I'm sure there's nothing wrong with it except for a few scratches. For your information *I'm* not hurt either, though you haven't had the decency to ask.'

'I didn't need to ask. I can tell you're all right by the state of your temper. Now, please let me see what can be done to get us out of this predicament.'

He climbed over her without ceremony and settled himself behind the wheel. The engine purred into life at the first try, but after shooting forward a few feet away from the bushes they were stuck fast in mud, and any further effort only drove the wheels in deeper. Hanna sat in stony silence while he tried various unsuccessful manoeuvres and got no response from the CB radio.

'The damp must have got into it,' he said. 'Not that anyone would turn out in this weather, but it would have helped if we could let people know where we are. Save them worrying.'

Meaning Jessica, of course. It was a wonder he hadn't brought her with him, but perhaps she had refused to come, knowing who it was that was causing so much trouble and wasting his time. He opened the door and tested the depth of the water. It went well over his shoes, which were already soaking from his trek across to get to Hanna. He removed them and tipped the water out, tying the laces together so that he could sling them round his neck. Luckily they were canvas.

'How good are you at carpentry?' he asked, 'because I reckon we shall have to build an ark.'

'My talent with a hammer and nails wouldn't even build us a raft, and if it meant staying afloat with just you for days on end I'd prefer to stay where I am.'

'Don't worry, things are not that bad.' He managed a grin. 'I couldn't stand it either, but not for the same reason.'

'I'm sorry I'm keeping you away from your precious Jessica,' she said, jumping to conclusions.

'So am I. I've a lot of things to say to her. But I do have Bill's car over there and all we have to do is get to it.' She started taking off her sandals. 'You needn't remove those,' he told her, 'I'm going to carry you across to the road.'

'You'll do no such thing,' she protested. 'I'll wade through it, the same as you.'

'What about the fire ants?'

She had several blisters on her feet from her encounter with them, but she would not be intimidated. Her memories of yesterday extended farther than the ants and she couldn't risk a repetition of what had followed.

'I'll just have to pray they've all drowned,' she said, and hurriedly stepped into the water before he could do anything about it.

He locked the car and pocketed his keys. It was not easy stumbling over the uneven ground, but she would not utter a single complaint. Sharp stones bit into her toes, scrubby bushes scratched her legs, and within minutes her dress was saturated and clinging to her skin. She scorned his offer of help, so he proceeded to ignore her and went on ahead, his long strides meeting up with only half the obstacles, and when he reached the road and looked back Hanna was still splashing her way across, sandals and bag held aloft. He threw back his head and gave a roar of laughter.

'Serves you right!' he shouted.

She paused a moment, glaring at him, and saw nothing funny in the situation. Her hair was drenched and rivulets of water ran down her forehead into her eyes. The sight of Ryan standing there laughing was more than she could bear. He looked like a pirate, bare-footed, trouser legs rolled up, wet shirt like a rag round his bronzed body, and a tangle of curls matted close to his head like a cap. No one would have recognised him. Hanna looked up at the dark clouds without a sign of a break in them, then down at the water where they were reflected, and was doubly despondent. Her expression matched the clouds exactly.

Still finding it amusing, he put his shoes down on the car bonnet and waded back to her. She ought to have realised his intention, but she was too worried at hearing a distant roll of thunder to guess what he was going to do. With a single swoop he scooped her off her feet and slung her over his shoulder like a sack of potatoes. She screamed, pummelled his back with her fists and kicked, but he took no notice.

'I know you won't be happy until I'm black and blue all over,' he said, and dumped her down beside the car. 'Thank goodness my bruises fade quickly.'

'I hate you, Ryan Donalson,' she cried. 'I don't think I've ever met anyone so destestable. I hate you!'

'Do you?' His low, sensuous voice mocked her and a half smile lingered on his lips. She shook herself like a puppy, showering him with spray from her hair, and there was a pain in her chest that took her breath away. Her back was against the car and there was no way she could have avoided him as he took her roughly into his arms. He held her face still with a firm hand, forcing her to look at him, and his mouth came down on hers in a cruel kiss that was more of an insult than anything. His body pressed against her, burning hot through the wet clothes, and she daren't move in case he became aware of the answering fire he awakened in her. Nor would she let herself acknowledge it. She held herself rigid, resisting him until his sheer physical strength made her yield. Surrender was heavenly. What did it matter if she returned his kisses with equal intensity? They might be quite incompatible when it came to ordinary dealing with each other, but the chemistry they generated was too powerful to be denied. His mouth became gentler, tracing a path across her eyelids, her nose, her neck, and then he questioned her again. 'Do you really hate me, Hanna?'

'Only when you deliberately provoke me. I don't know how anyone could put up with you.'

'I rarely give anyone a chance,' he said. He looked up at the sky, letting the rain pour down on his unprotected face. 'Don't you just love the rain? I'll bet you've never been kissed in a deluge like this before. You'll remember it for the rest of your life.'

'Or try to forget it.'

'Come off it, Hanna. You got as much pleasure out of that as I did, and whenever it rains on you and Jay Caldwell you'll think about me.'

It was a derisory statement, delivered like a parting shot as he opened the car door and got inside. When she made no move to do the same, he asked: 'Are you coming with me, or staying there?'

He was right. There had never been anything so exhilarating as that kiss in the rain, and like him she
suddenly found excitement in just being out in such
weather. She blinked and rubbed her hand across her
eyes because her vision was blurred. Who was Jay
Caldwell? Right now there were only two people in the
world, herself and Ryan.

She walked round the car and got in the other side.
'We're making rather a mess of Bill's upholstery.'

'What do you expect, with the mess we're in?' He
turned to her and for a moment the mocking light died
in his eyes and it was as if there was something important he wanted to say. But then he flicked his head and
looked away again. 'It'll soon dry.'

It was difficult to turn in the road, but the car was
not so large as the Buick and Ryan handled it with
comparative ease. He drove slowly, the tyres whining
along the wet surface, and in places where the water
was deeper waves fanned out in their wake. They had
gone less than a mile when conditions deteriorated. The
rumble of thunder Hanna had heard was a prelude to
the returning storm. At the first flash of lightning she
covered her eyes with both hands, and so missed the
teasing smile Ryan directed at her.

Rain on the windscreen sounded like incessant gunfire
and it was almost impossible to see out, but under the
trees there was some respite and he pulled in to wait for
the worst of it to pass. It was then they saw the house.
It was close to the road in a clearing, more like a shack
than anything, but there were curtains at the window
and the door stood open. There was a fresh crash of
thunder and Hanna turned to Ryan, burying her face
against him involuntarily, and his arms enfolded her.
She was trembling with fear.

Someone shouted from the doorway, 'Y'come on in
now, do y' hear?' and an old man was beckoning them.

It was getting dark. The hours had passed in trauma

since she had started out and she hadn't counted them. Afternoon had become evening without her being aware of it and it was not only the storm clouds that darkened the sky.

'Come on,' said Ryan. 'We can't stay here.'

He picked her up like a child and carried her through flood water to where the old man stood, welcoming them inside.

'There now, ain't that better than being out there? Where you from? You sure enough ain't crossed the river on that ole ferry with the river this high?'

'We got lost,' Hanna explained.

'Been to visit family,' Ryan elaborated. 'We were hoping to get back to Port Gibson.'

'Well, you won't be wise to try tonight.' The old man scratched his grizzled head. 'Who're your folks? We don't get many strangers round these parts, and can't say I've ever set eyes on you two before.'

'The Caldwells,' Hanna said quickly, knowing she had to produce a name or he might become suspicious.

He busied himself lighting an oil lamp that stood on an ancient cane table. 'Electricity failed a couple of hours ago. Tell you what, though, I've some cans of beer still cool enough to drink. Caldwell? Yeah, I know. English woman with two boys, married Jake Caldwell. If you want you can have my daughter's trailer for the night. She's away right now trying to mend a quarrel with her husband. Never did think he was right for her.'

Hanna started to protest. 'No, we can't . . .'

But Ryan's voice was louder. 'That's very kind of you. We'll pay for the use of it.'

'You're welcome. Now sit yourselves down while I get the beer and show you my carvings.'

Feeling as if all the air had been knocked out of her, Hanna sat down on an old settle, the only seat in the room apart from a large rocking chair. Ryan went to give a hand with the beer. For several minutes he stood in the lean-to kitchen that led off the main room, giving the old man all his attention, and her throat constricted with emotion. The strange light accentuated his male cragginess, his tall figure that curved under the low ceiling. Then he came and sat next to her on the settle. It was narrow, meant for two small people, not one his size, and there was no way she could avoid contact.

'That's mighty prim accents you got,' the old man commented, pouring Hanna's beer into a glass as courtesy towards a lady demanded. He pulled the ring of his own can and tipped it to his mouth, expecting Ryan to do the same. 'I'd say you was English.'

'That's right,' she said, and his face lit up.

For a while he talked. Like all lonely people he took advantage of having someone to talk to and words flowed from him like a burst dam. There was hardly any need to answer, and Ryan did it for both of them. Hanna lost the thread of what he was saying altogether. She was too conscious of Ryan's thigh pressed close against hers, the warm, damp smell of him, and when he leaned forward to take one of the carvings the old man handed him his arm touched against her breast, lingering there, she was sure, with intent. He must feel how her heart throbbed. The thought of spending a night alone with him in a trailer made her head spin dizzily.

'I guess you're a pretty girl when you're dry,' the man was saying. He squinted at her through old eyes that had probably squinted at more than seventy summer suns. 'How's about you going over to the trailer to dry off and get something ready for your husband to eat? There's a calor gas stove and some food to use up.'

She opened her mouth, attempting to put things right. 'He's not . . .'

But once more Ryan interrupted. 'My wife doesn't like storms, but it seems to have gone over again.'

'Sure has. Come on, little lady.' He opened the door of the lean-to and showed her the trailer, set just a few yards from the house under a huge magnolia tree.

'Door's open, and the path ain't too wet.'

'Ryan?' She looked at him beseechingly, but his expression was bland.

'I'll be with you in a moment,' he told her.

'When we've finished the beer,' said the old man.

It was much bigger inside the trailer than she had imagined and even in the fading light she could see how beautifully it was kept. She felt like an intruder as she wandered round the room and explored the corridor leading to a bathroom and bedroom. It was hot. With the power failure there was no air-conditioning and she realised how much people out here relied on it, but it would only have made it worse if she had opened windows.

She stood in the bathroom, mesmerised by the number of bottles and jars that took up so much of the small space, and belonged to a woman she didn't know. She had no right to be here, and she was ashamed of the way she hadn't contradicted Ryan when he had called her his wife. He'd trapped her. But wasn't she a willing victim, and how was she going to escape, unless she was fool enough to try and take another car from him? She would just have to keep out of his way as much as possible. There was a mirror over the sink and she caught sight of herself unexpectedly. No wonder the old man hadn't been sure whether she was pretty or not! She looked like a Persian cat that had just been dragged out of a pond.

Without any more hesitation she peeled off her clothes, turned on the water and climbed into the bath. There was a bottle of shampoo on the side which she used, followed by a small quantity of scented oil, then she sank back in the luxurious warm water with as much enjoyment as if she was staying at the best hotel. The soothing effect was so wonderful it made her sleepy and she lay soaking longer than she intended. It meant scrambling out and wrapping herself in the largest towel she could find when she heard Ryan's voice outside.

'You and your wife can bed down there as cosy as you like.'

'I'll square up with you in the morning,' said Ryan. 'And thank you again.'

They opened the door. 'Ain't no smell of cookin' yet.' The old man sniffed the air. 'What kind of wife you got, mister? Ain't she a good cook?'

'The best,' said Ryan. 'Her coffee's out of this world.' And he came inside and shut the door.

Hanna remembered his reaction to her coffee the only time he had tasted it in London. Well, he wouldn't get any better tonight, because there was only the instant variety to be found in the store cupboard. She lit the calor gas lamp, bringing the room to life, and picked up a rolling pin that was by the cooker.

'I've left you some bath water and there's another towel. I'll hang our clothes on the line out here and they should be dry by morning. This,' brandishing the rolling pin, 'is in case you try any of your tricks. I assure you I'll use it if I have to, and it's a lot harder than my bag.'

'Message received and understood, Mrs Donalson.'

'How dare you call me that! I haven't forgiven you yet for letting that man think we were married.'

Ryan pulled off his shirt. The lamplight glowed on his brown skin, shadowing the dark hair on his chest and arms. 'Don't worry, I've never yet taken a girl against her will. Now, it would be a good idea if you do something about food while I'm tidying myself up.'

He issued the order as if he was talking to a junior on the studio floor, making her rebellious, but she curbed a sharp reply and set about lighting the stove. The smell was awful and she had difficulty adjusting the flame, but she found a pan, some sausages and bacon in the rapidly defrosting fridge, and managed to have a fairly presentable meal ready for dishing up by the time he came back, even though it was somewhat charred at the edges.

The second towel was tied firmly round his middle

and he handed her his lightweight trousers to hang over the line with his shirt. The thought that he probably had nothing on under the towel brought her out in goose pimples and she wished her own clothes were dry.

'I'm sorry it's a burnt offering,' she said, 'but I've never used one of those stoves before.' She put the plate in front of him, keeping well to her side of the table.

Ryan smiled ruefully. 'Jessica would have conjured up sausage risotto with side salad from that lot.'

Hanna's eyes blazed and her lips firmed into a belligerent line. 'And no doubt she would have bedded down with you right cosy,' she goaded him. 'Well, I'm afraid it's me you're stuck with here and you'll have to put up with it. I didn't ask you to come looking for me.'

'Han—na!' His tone was apologetic. 'Can't we stop fighting, just for tonight anyway? This is very nice and I'm not complaining. All I meant was Jessica turns everything into fancy dishes, elaborates things generally. I'd much rather have this.'

Slightly appeased, she sat down and started eating. She hadn't realised how hungry she was and the fat American sausages tasted very good. Ryan seemed to think so, too, the way he devoured them with genuine enjoyment. But it was unnerving sitting opposite him at table, having cooked him a meal. It felt too natural.

'How did you know where to look for me?' she asked.

He finished the last piece of sausage and pushed the plate aside. 'That was good, Hanna, thank you.' The rolls were hard, but he broke one and buttered it. 'It was some time before I went back to my room and then I couldn't find my keys. Everyone had gone by then, so I went to see if I'd left them in the car, but that was missing, too. As luck would have it Bill came back for something and told me how you and Jessica had had words, so we put two and two together. I phoned your aunt and she'd just got back from the hospital, but she said her neighbour saw you, so I borrowed Bill's car and came after you. I knew you'd come to Windsor Castle, and I could see the storm brewing.'

'You knew I'd come to Windsor Castle?'

'Oh, yes.' His eyes softened. 'It's a special place, and yesterday was a special day, wasn't it?'

Hanna couldn't look at him. Her defences were crumbling and he mustn't see how vulnerable she was. It would be all too easy to let the comforting atmosphere of this lamplit room complete the illusion that they belonged together like this. She had to fan the flames of anger.

'If it was so special for you, too, why did you turn traitor and let Jessica believe so many dreadful things about me? She said I blackmailed you into taking me along so that I could see my relations on the cheap. It was the other way round if there was any blackmailing done, and you know it!'

'I never said that to her,' Ryan assured her. 'She makes things up to suit herself.'

'Well, it didn't sound like that. She accused me of stealing her work, and ... and ...' She couldn't say 'and the only man she had ever loved' without it seeming as if she had tried to do just that, so she changed the words. 'And she told me how you both laughed over the scene I wrote. Okay, so you found it funny, but you knew I wasn't a writer when you asked me to do it.'

A kettle was boiling and she made coffee, sprinkling it with powdered milk before thrusting it in front of him defiantly. 'My coffee isn't Espresso standard either, as you well know.'

He put sugar in it and stirred it slowly, then sipped it as if it was the best he'd tasted. At least he was trying to be nice, which brought on a twinge of guilt.

'Hanna, I didn't laugh at your script.' He was frowning and looked at her seriously from beneath those craggy brows.

'It doesn't matter if you did. I'm without a job anyway.' She spoke bitterly. 'It's all been quite a shattering experience coming out here with you, and I never want to go through anything like it again.'

'That's a pity, because when Jessica voiced the fact that she was firing you I said I had other plans for you myself. I agreed it wouldn't be wise for you to work together.'

Hanna got up from the table and started clearing away the things. There was a small sink in the kitchen area at the back of the trailer and she stacked them beside it.

'Plans? I don't want to know anything about plans involving you, Ryan Donalson. I can't wait to get back home so that I never have to see you again!'

She had her back to him, which was just as well because he would have seen there were foolish tears in her eyes. Whatever her opinion of him, nothing altered the fact that life without him would be unbearable. She would even miss their fights. He had brought drama, glamour and excitement into each day, and even when sparks were flying and he was at his most overbearing, she loved him.

'Hanna.' He came up behind her. 'You have a wonderful feel for writing. Maybe you need to learn the techniques of it, but won't you at least come and work with me when we get back?'

She was so surprised she turned without thinking, and found herself in his arms. Knowing that if she stayed there he would kiss her and she would lack all resistance, she gave him an unexpected push that made him stagger backwards. The trailer floor shuddered and cups jingled on their hooks.

'Don't try and get round me!' she exclaimed furiously. 'If you think spending the night here with me is going to be a change from spending last night with Jessica you've got another think coming! I don't want any favours from you, and I haven't put the rolling pin away.'

She filled the sink with water which was cool after

running it off for the bath, and scrubbed at the dishes to try and get the grease off. Ryan picked up a cloth and waited patiently to dry them. Luckily she couldn't see the aggravating smile that turned the corners of his lips upwards.

'Why do you assume I take different women to bed each night?' he asked, quite casually. 'Vicki, Jessica. And you have the conceit to think I even might consider you!'

Colour flooded her cheeks. She had overstepped the mark and made herself look ridiculous. She emptied the sink and wiped it clean, saying nothing because she was struggling with tears again. The wretch was forever putting her at a disadvantage! She went past him and he made no effort to detain her this time, found a brush in her bag and began brushing her hair vigorously. The action brought a measure of relief and she gradually became calmer.

'I'm sorry,' she said. 'I've been meaning to apologise to you about Vicki. I heard what really happened.'

He came over and tilted up her chin. 'You were jealous, my little spitfire.'

'I was no such thing!' There he went again, tormenting, getting amusement out of inciting her. 'And if you think that, then your conceit is a damn sight worse then mine!' She hitched the towel round her more tightly so that she could lift her arms and knot her hair up out of the way. It was stifling in the trailer and she felt she could hardly breathe. Certainly she couldn't stay near him a minute longer. 'It's been a long, difficult day. There's only one bed and I intend to have it. I hope you can find somewhere reasonably comfortable to sleep. Goodnight.'

She went into the bedroom, taking her bra and pants and waist slip with her. They were dry and she felt safer when they were on. But she was not really tired. The exhaustion she felt was purely mental and she began to think she would never be able to relax again. She looked out of the window and the sky was inky black, no sign of moon or stars. But the rain had stopped and there was no sound except the dripping of moisture from the trees on to the roof.

She lay on the bed, staring at the ceiling for a long time, and there was an ache in her stomach that wouldn't go away—a curling, insistent ache that got worse every time she thought about tomorrow and leaving Vicksburg. Losing Ryan for ever. Yes, that was the real cause of it. The ache was a longing to have him here beside her on the big double bed. Why was she so bound by convention that she couldn't suggest sharing the bed just for this one night? Tomorrow he was going back to Jessica and she would never have another chance to be with him.

But he didn't want her. He had said so.

In the early hours the remnants of the storm returned, fierce in its final onslaught, and Hanna awoke to find the bedroom suffused with brilliant light that flickered with bluish white intensity, magnifying everything before the thunder crack deafened her. Too frightened to scream, she buried herself under the single sheet that was all the covering she had needed, and waited for her last moment to come.

'It's all right, Hanna, it won't hurt you.' Ryan gently pulled the cover away from her face and drew her up into his arms. 'The sky's clearing. It's moving away at last.'

She was feverish with the heat, but her teeth were chattering and she clung to him, hiding her face against his chest as another flash of lightning came, less spectacular than the first. He held her like that until she lost track of time, and gradually her shivering stopped. His expert fingers knew which tension spots to massage in her neck and she relaxed against him with a contented sigh as delicious rippling sensations chased down her spine. There was no place in the world she would rather be than cradled here in his arms, and her own arms crept around him, pressing him even closer. For a while he let her need of him take command, then he carefully unlocked her hands and put her from him.

'Do you know we missed a party tonight?' he said lightly. 'It was the end of location celebration. I guess if anyone's sober enough they'll send a search party out looking for us.'

'They won't find us,' was Hanna's drowsy reply.

She lay back beneath the sheet and smiled up at him, her hair loose again and spread across the pillow. A pale dawn light was creeping in to show her the hunger in his eyes. He leaned over and she waited for the pressure of his mouth to blot out every single thought and send her spinning into mindless ecstasy, but he only looked at her with that strange yearning she had seen once before.

'I want you, Hanna,' he murmured. 'I want you more than I've ever wanted anything.'

'I want you, too,' she whispered. 'It's all right, Ryan.'

But he sat up and turned away from her. 'No. It wouldn't be fair.'

She wanted to scream at him that nothing was ever fair. What did tomorrow matter, or all the other tomorrows? They were here, now, and they needed each other. She didn't care if she was just another girl to add to his list of conquests. She loved him, and wanted this night to remember for the rest of her life, because it was all there would ever be. But she was too choked to do more than utter his name.

'Ryan . . .'

He was silent for a while, and emotions chased across his proud, handsome face as he battled within himself for control, and she wished she had the courage to tell him again there was no need.

'A couple of weeks ago,' he said, 'something happened that shattered my orderly existence. I didn't think there was any woman in the world capable of doing it, but she did. I want to tell her how much I love her, but there are too many complications, and I'm not going to add to those complications. So, please, try to understand.'

When he looked at her again she could only see him through a mist of tears. Oh, yes, she understood very well. Jessica's betrayal, her marriage to Alistair had made his world collapse, and it was like a miracle she had been returned to him. Nothing must happen to spoil this second chance of happiness. And though her own heart was breaking into a thousand fragments, she had to be glad that everything was turning out right for him.

'Now I'm going to stay here for the rest of the night with the cover between us so that you needn't be frightened any more.'

And he lay beside her on top of the sheet and tucked her head comfortably into the crook of his arm.

CHAPTER ELEVEN

WHEN she awoke the sun was shining. At first she couldn't think where she was as the strange bedroom swam into focus and unfamiliar shapes met her eyes. She hadn't even noticed what was in the room last night.

Then she remembered Ryan and turned to touch him, but the place beside her was empty and she was alone in the big bed. If only he had stayed! To have woken up next to him just once in her life would have been joy beyond compare. But no sooner had the thought entered her mind than she rejected it. She didn't regret the opportunity that was lost. If Ryan had made love to her she would have been totally committed to loving him, and with no hope of having that love returned what use was it to torture herself with the knowledge of what might have been? His own restraint was so completely unexpected it filled her with grudging admiration, until an alarming possibility replaced it with humiliation. Had her fear-induced state last night made her issue an invitation he really had no interest in accepting. His opinion of her must have sunk to an all-time low. She curled up in despair, ashamed of herself and afraid to face him.

But she couldn't continue hiding away from him when he was her only means of getting back to Vicksburg, so she pushed back the sheet and took a deep breath. There was the most appetising smell of cooked breakfast coming from the other room and she found she was hungry. She slipped into her clothes, stood a moment to gather her courage, then decided to brazen it out and say nothing about what had happened in the night. That way both of them would be spared embarrassment.

'Good morning,' he said, wielding a wooden spatula over the frying pan as though it was what he was used to doing. 'I was just going to bring you some coffee. There doesn't appear to be such a thing as tea.'

'Coffee will do fine,' she said. 'Would you like me to do anything?'

'Only sit down and eat *my* burnt offering. I don't seem to be much better with the stove than you were.' He was being kind. The bacon and sausages were cooked to perfection. 'We must start back as soon as we can. I'm going to drop you off at your aunt's, get someone from a garage to rescue my car, and drive back to Vicksburg to finalise everything there. I shall want you back at the motel by lunchtime. Our flight leaves Jackson at seven.'

His tone was businesslike, instructions issued clearly and precisely, not to be questioned. Only Hanna had never been part of his working life and she found the audacity to contradict.

'I can go back for the car. Either that or I'll drive Bill's car and you can get it.'

Ryan's brow clouded ominously and his eyes flashed sparks of annoyance. 'You will not touch either of the cars. I'm not having you drive alone on these roads again, so don't suggest it.'

'I'm sorry, it just seemed a waste of time.'

'It's a pity you didn't think of that yesterday.'

They ate in silence, then she dared to question him again. 'What if Jay asks me to stay on?'

The frown got even darker. 'Whatever you decide to do about your boy-friend is up to you, but you'll be coming back to England on the same flight as everyone else. You can return here later if you want to.'

She had never heard his voice so coldly authoritative and any further argument was impossible, even if she had felt inclined. But her only reason for speaking of Jay had been to cover her dejection and let Ryan think last night's weakness had meant no more to her than it had to him. She was not going to let him guess for an instant that Jay was no more to her than an affectionate cousin and would have to be told so as soon as she saw him.

When she stepped outside the morning was lovely. Sunshine tipped the wet leaves with diamonds and the creamy magnolia blooms glowed with waxen beauty among the dark green sheen. There was even a peculiar charm about the shack with its wilderness surroundings softened by a heat haze. She had cleared everything up and left the trailer as tidy as when they arrived, and Ryan gave the old man a quantity of dollars far exceeding what was needed to replace the food they had used. Hardly crediting his luck, he waved them off regretfully, repeating over and over that they must come back and meet his daughter.

The water had cleared from the road as quickly as it had flooded and only the freshness of the creeper-covered trees and the pungent, earthy smell gave credence to yesterday's storm. Ryan had nothing to say to Hanna and she sat beside him so inwardly agitated she wanted to shut her eyes and blot out all the memories that caused her pain. But if she did that she would waste the precious minutes that were all that was left of her time alone with him, and she had to absorb every detail to store away so that the bleak days ahead were bearable. The way his hands rested on the wheel, the shape of his fingernails, the set of his head, his mouth with a promised smile almost visible. Oh, yes, he could smile now. He was on his way to see Jessica.

No wonder Hanna's nerves were quaking. There was so much unpleasantness to be faced in the next few hours there didn't seem to be a single ray of light on the horizon. First of all she had to see Jay and tell him as kindly as possible that she couldn't even consider marrying him. What would he and Aunt Rachael think when she arrived at this time of the morning, stepping out of Ryan Donalson's car with her dress all crumpled? He might even think he had had a lucky escape when she told him of her decision.

And then there was Jessica. Having experienced her rage when it was directed at her quite unjustly, Hanna dreaded the thought of another volley for which there was at least some cause. For Ryan's sake it was to be hoped she believed him when he told her the truth about last night. In self-defence he would probably make a joke of it, playing on the innocence of the situation and making out he had been dealing with nothing more than a child who had run off in a tantrum. Yesterday the thought of him doing that would have infuriated her anew, but today she was more understanding.

It was still quite early when he pulled up outside Aunt Rachael's house, but it looked as if they already had a visitor because another car was parked in the entrance.

'Thank you,' she said awkwardly, before getting out. 'It was good of you to come and look for me, and in case I don't get a chance to talk to you alone again I want you to know it's been a wonderful experience coming to America with your television company. And I'm sorry if I've annoyed you, but . . .'

Her hands were shaking as she opened the door, and even then she had to turn to him once more.

'I'll miss you so much,' she said in a husky whisper, careless of what he read into the words.

She tried not to meet his eyes, afraid he would see tears gathering. She wanted to delay the moment of parting so that she could store every single impression of him, but there was nothing more she could capture, and common sense told her to get it over quickly. But he cupped her chin with his hand, delaying her himself, and a strange light burned in the depths of those greyish-brown eyes.

'Hanna, don't decide anything too hurriedly. Promise me.' He seemed to be actually appealing to her.

'I already have decided . . .' she began.

'Then remember the mistake Jessica made in marrying

someone she hardly knew. It may seem as if you've known Jay Caldwell a long time because he's your cousin, but the time you've really known him amounts only to a few days.'

'But I . . .'

'I've got to get back to Vicksburg,' Ryan interrupted. 'Make sure Jay knows the time I've stipulated *you* have to be there. I don't want to have to make this trip again.'

And with that he leaned over and pushed open the door so that she had to get out. She went up the path to the house without another glance, not even turning to watch him drive away.

The door was standing open and she could hear voices inside, young laughter, a radio belting out pop music. She called and at first no one heard. Then a young girl came through to the kitchen and saw her.

'Hi,' she said. 'You looking for someone?'

'My aunt,' said Hanna, 'but I don't suppose she's up yet.' She went inside.

'Why, you must be cousin Hanna. They've told me all about you. Hey, Leigh, it's Hanna!'

Mystified, Hanna went through to the kitchen. 'Are you Leigh's girl-friend?'

'No, Jay's,' the girl said. 'I'm Mandy-Sue. We've known each other since High School, but I've been away for a couple of months staying with my grandparents in Iowa. I thought I'd better come back before someone else grabbed him.'

She was a pretty girl, with bright blue eyes and heavy fair hair cut like a glossy cap that shone when she moved her head. She wore shorts and her long brown legs were good enough to win a competition. Leigh came from the bathroom, carrying a radio and trying to towel his hair with one hand.

'Hi, Hanna,' he said, without showing any surprise at seeing her. 'Come on in and grab yourself some break-fast.' He put the radio down and slapped Mandy-Sue's bottom with a familiarity that proved they were old friends. She squealed and dodged away.

'Thanks, but I've had some. I really want to see Jay,' said Hanna.

At that moment Jay appeared, rubbing his eyes. 'Mandy-Sue, do you have to wake people this early, and this loud? I like to come round slowly in the mornings.' He stopped abruptly, seeing Hanna, and the T-shirt he was pulling on remained halfway. 'Hanna, I was coming over directly. There was no need for you to come all this way.'

His face was a picture, consternation, confusion, could it even be guilt, all mirrored there because she had arrived and been greeted by Mandy-Sue.

'Ryan brought me,' Hanna explained. 'We leave this evening . . .'

'I know. I've been in a panic. I phoned the motel last night and no one knew where you were. Then Mandy-Sue arrived and the weather got so bad Momma said she could stop over and sleep on the couch. But where were you?'

'It's a long story,' said Hanna, and had vivid memories of a night she had spent on a couch herself only a short time ago. What a lot had happened since! 'I came to say goodbye, Jay. Can I go through and see Aunt Rachael?'

He followed her out of the kitchen, leaving the others to stare after them as he closed the door, and his agitation made him dart in front to delay her.

'Please, Hanna, please don't be angry,' he implored her. 'I can explain everything. Mandy-Sue doesn't mean anything to me any more. Please listen!'

She felt years older than him. He was like a puppy that had been naughty, gazing at her with soulful eyes that begged forgiveness, yet there was nothing to forgive.

'I am listening, Jay,' she said gently. 'I like Mandy-Sue and I'm glad she's here. It makes it easier to say I can't marry you. It's all been a game really, hasn't it? You'll agree with me in a while.' She put a finger over his lips when fresh protests were about to rush forth. 'But thank you for asking me. I'll never forget you.'

She tiptoed up to kiss his cheek, then hurried away before he could stop her.

Aunt Rachael was sitting up in bed, her usually bright face clouded with worry at hearing the commotion outside and not being able to get up to find out what was going on. When she saw Hanna the frown cleared, but Hanna looked so troubled she didn't wait to greet her verbally, just held out her arms to her. Hanna flew to them, dropping on her knees beside the bed, and it was like coming home to her mother. She hadn't realised how hard it had been to hold back tears, and once they started to flow she sobbed for several minutes, comforted by her aunt's understanding silence and tender hands. But Aunt Rachael knew when enough was enough.

'There, there, child,' she murmured, 'no man is worth breaking your heart over like this. It can't be that son of mine that's making you take on so, even though Mandy-Sue's turned up. No, it's that other one, isn't it? Ryan Donalson.'

'Yes,' said Hanna, on a gulping breath. 'I love him, Aunt Rachael.'

'And he doesn't want to know. Well . . . it happens to us all at some time.' She paused a moment, then made Hanna look at her. 'Are you sure he doesn't care?'

'Yes. Jessica came back to him yesterday.' She told her aunt the whole story, right up to what happened yesterday, leaving out nothing except the fact that she had spent the night alone with Ryan in the trailer. She said the old man had put them up, and left it at that.

'Seems to me that man's more complicated than one of his television plots,' was her aunt's comment. 'Not knowing him all that well I'm no fair judge, but if he can't see that you're worth two of that flighty creature he's been holding a candle to all these years, then he deserves to suffer. I'm guess I'm prejudiced, honey, but I have a feeling you ought not to give up altogether. He sounded right bothered when he phoned up and found you weren't here. We all thought you'd gone back to Vicksburg, but when he called in and said you hadn't, he looked like a man who cares a whole lot more than he'd let on.'

'Ryan came here!'

'He did, honey.' Aunt Rachael smiled. 'And if I'd been your age I guess I'd feel exactly the way you do about him.'

Hanna sighed. 'He only cares because he's responsible for me until we get back to England. He thinks I'm a dreadful nuisance and he can't wait to pay me off and see the back of me.'

'Well, you know him better than I do, and all I can say is perhaps someone better will come along.'

'No, they won't,' said Hanna with conviction.

Aunt Rachael looked into her eyes steadily, and patted her hand. 'Have faith, Hanna.' She gave her niece a long, affectionate hug, then set her away from her. 'Now I'm going to get up. It takes me a while, so you go through to the bathroom and tidy your face, then find the boys and have coffee or a Coke. I've lots of things to give you for your mother, and messages for you to take. Tell her she's got to bring your father over here before the year's out. And I want *you* to come back and stay with us just as soon as you can, and for as long as you can. We love you, child.'

'I love you, too, Aunt Rachael,' said Hanna, her eyes misting dangerously again, 'Can I help you to get up?'

'No. I'm used to doing things my own way.' She pushed back the covers. 'Oh, and Hanna, I'll ask Leigh to drive you back to Vicksburg later. It might be best.'

'Thank you. I'm sure you're right.'

Leigh was in a talkative mood and kept up an endless

flow of chatter all the way to Vicksburg. Hanna had never seen him so volatile and wondered whether it had anything to do with the return of Mandy-Sue, in which case there was going to be some brotherly rivalry. To her relief he didn't wait for or seem to expect many answers, and she let the chatter drift over her head as she faced her next problem: Jessica. She had come through the first of her ordeals much easier than she had expected, but she was really dreading the next few hours. She couldn't avoid her. Even if she wasn't around when she got to the motel she would see her at the airport, and confrontation there in front of a huge crowd was too awful to contemplate. She already knew that time and place were immaterial to Jessica if she thought she had a score to settle. The best thing, Hanna decided, would be to find out which room she was in and approach her in private. With a bit of luck perhaps Ryan would have seen her already and put things right between them, then no further explanations would be necessary. It was too much to hope that an apology might be offered for yesterday.

'I'm not going to let her scare me,' Hanna said out loud.

'Who's that?' asked Leigh, pausing in mid-flow to wonder what on earth she was talking about.

'Jessica Franklin—er—Kerby. No, Franklin, soon to be Donalson.'

Leigh shrugged. 'Are you feeling okay?'

'Yes, I think so,' she said.

Her cousin dropped her at the motel entrance, too embarrassed to give her more than a brief farewell hug. And then she was alone.

There was no air of impending mass departure yet. The foyer was empty except for two suitcases left at one side for collection. They looked familiar and Hanna recognised them as the two she had helped Jessica to pack before the wedding. The sight of them brought on a feeling of panic, but she stiffened her back and went to the desk, intending to ring to ask for Jessica's room number. But before she could do so the door from the lounge burst open and Jessica sailed in.

'Hanna, I've been looking everywhere for you. Where have you been?'

Hanna turned, her face pale but her resolve undiminished. 'I had to say goodbye to my aunt.'

'Darling, I know, but I needed you. I'm in such a terrible rush and you've got to do something for me.'

'But I . . .' Hanna began, too astounded to do anything but stare.

'Oh, I know I was beastly to you yesterday, but you never take any notice of me when I'm feeling like that, do you? It's what makes you such a perfect secretary. Now, darling, I'm afraid I've got to leave you to deliver a message for me.'

'I'm sorry, but I understood I was no longer working for you.' The lump in Hanna's throat felt as big as a rockery stone as she interrupted her. Jessica's eyes were sparkling, her cheeks bright, her step light. Every movement spoke of love rekindled, and obviously Ryan had settled everything to her satisfaction. Well, good for him, but that didn't mean all was forgiven and forgotten, and Hanna had no intention of falling back into her old job as if nothing had changed.

'Hanna, dar—ling!' Jessica's eyes widened in almost believable surprise, then she darted to Hanna and clasped her hands impetuously between her own. 'Please, please, please don't take all I said yesterday to heart. I couldn't bear it, not now I'm so deliriously happy. The most wonderful thing has happened!'

'Yes,' said Hanna. 'I'm very pleased for you.' If her voice lacked enthusiasm it was doubtful whether Jessica would even notice. 'Ryan's very lucky after all.'

'Ryan?' Jessica exclaimed. 'He's got nothing to do with it. Like I said, I'm in a tearing hurry and I want you to give him a message because I just don't have to time to do it myself.' She broke off and gave Hanna a beseeching look. 'Oh, darling, I know it's a rotten job and you had to do it before, but this time it won't be so bad. He's over the initial shock by now.'

A dawning fear crept up on Hanna. 'You mean you haven't seen Ryan?'

'That's what I'm trying to tell you. I know it's absolutely naughty of me, darling, but since I had the phone call from Alistair it's been one mad rush to get things arranged, and now I'm waiting for the taxi to take me to the airport.'

'Alistair?' gasped Hanna.

'He phoned to apologise for the *terrible* row we had—said it was all his fault. Wasn't that darling of him? And his paper is sending him to New York to cover a story tonight and he wants me to meet him there. Oh, I just can't wait to see him again!'

Hanna's heart was beating so fast she felt as if she had been running.

'You can't be serious about expecting *me* to tell Ryan? Jessica! Of all the callous, cruel, unfeeling women, I think you're the worst I've ever met!'

To cap it all, Jessica laughed. 'I know, darling, but he'll understand. Just tell him I hope everything, just everything, comes out right for him. Oh, thank the lord, my taxi's here.' She gave Hanna a quick, hard squeeze and kissed her cheek. 'Take care of him, Hanna. Goodbye. See you in London!'

She was gone like a whirlwind, and in the aftermath Hanna was left feeling more shattered than she had ever been in her life. The taxi driver came into the foyer to collect Jessica's luggage and gave her an odd look, obviously wondering if she was ill, and it was as much as she could do to reassure him when he enquired.

With leaden feet she went up to her room, closed the door and sank down on the bed. Jessica had done it again, left her to give Ryan devastating news that she was too cowardly to impart herself. Only this time it was so much worse because instead of dealing with a stranger and feeling just passing sympathy, she was involved on her own account. Too deeply involved by far. Loving Ryan, yet knowing what high hopes he had had of a reconciliation with Jessica, her heart ached with actual physical pain. She didn't know how he would take it.

She ought to have refused point blank to pass on the message. There was no reason why she should do anything for Jessica. But it was not for her that she would be doing it. She had to warn Ryan so that he didn't discover what she had done unexpectedly, in a public place perhaps where his feelings must be completely hidden. Damn Jessica! No, that was too mild an expletive to express the way she felt about her. This morning she had managed to find some excuses for the way she had behaved yesterday, but she would never ever forgive her for the way she treated Ryan. Not that he couldn't take care of himself very well, but Hanna knew now something of his deep inner feelings, and pictured the clipped arrogance that would cover them.

That she would be in with a chance of winning him herself did occur to her, but she dismissed the idea immediately. She would never play second fiddle to Jessica, and that was what it would mean. There was no knowing when Jessica would have the next row with Alistair and come running back to cause more trouble. It would probably happen with ridiculous regularity.

She didn't know how long she had been lying there staring at the ceiling when she heard footsteps pass her door. Ryan. His stride was purposeful and she guessed he had been down to see that his car was all right for the drive back to Jackson. She got up slowly and looked in the mirror. She was still wearing the crumpled dress that had taken such a soaking yesterday. She certainly couldn't go to see him looking like that.

Most of her clothes were packed, but she took out the trousers and jacket she had bought in Vicksburg, decided they gave her an air of chic regardless of how she was feeling, and were suitable for travellling. No good going home looking as drab as she felt. The pull of the brush through her hair did wonders for her morale.

'Right, Hanna Ballantyne, here we go again,' she said to her reflection, and gave her chin the customary lift. She had to face him and the sooner it was over the better.

Her tap on his door was crisp, businesslike, and when he called out to come in she did so briskly. He was emptying the cupboard and pushing his things into the holdall with a carelessness that made her want to tip it all out and do the job herself.

'I've been expecting you,' he said. 'Where have you been all this time? Do you know how much the bill is for the car? No, I'd better not tell you. I threatened to give it to you to pay. Can you think of any reason why I shouldn't?'

She was taken by surprise, her mind too occupied with more important things, and she stammered, 'Yes—er—no. I don't know.'

Ryan straightened up and looked at her squarely. 'That's not like you, Hanna. You usually have a very definite answer for everything. What would you say if I asked you to marry me?'

He was being flippant. She bit her lip, sorrow for him welling up and threatening to spill over, and to hide it she managed a sharp retort.

'I'd probably accept just to spite you.' She leaned back against the door. 'Ryan, there's something I have to tell you.'

'That's settled, then,' he said, ignoring her last remark. 'Let's seal it with a loving kiss, shall we?'

He came towards her, his eyes mocking, taunting her as always.

'Please, Ryan, you've got to listen!'

She dodged sideways, but he caught her because there

was nowhere she could go other than towards the bed. His arms trapped her just firmly enough to ensure that escape was impossible, and allowed her to struggle like a little bird until it became futile, laughing when she feigned anger. Then he claimed her unresisting mouth, kissing her possessively for what seemed an eternity, until her response left no doubt of the passion he aroused. When he lifted his head the only expression in his eyes was too wonderful, too revealing to be true, and she swam dizzily within the circle of his arms so that he had to hold her even tighter.

'It's been nearly twenty-four hours since I kissed you,' he murmured. 'I don't know how I've survived that long.' And a little while later he said: 'Now, what was it you wanted to tell me?'

Hanna shook her head, trying to think clearly. All this nonsense had made her forget why she had come.

'It's Jessica,' she said hazily.

'I don't want to hear another word about her.'

'But, Ryan,' she extricated herself at last and put a reasonably safe distance between them, 'she's gone back to Alistair.'

'I know,' said Ryan. 'I arranged it.'

She protested, 'I don't believe it!'

He looked at his watch and gave her a wicked, teasing smile before sauntering over to his packing. 'Okay, I won't tell you.'

She didn't know what to make of it, and after watching for a moment in exasperation, waiting in vain for him to do some explaining, she went over and barred his way to the cupboard. 'Stop tormenting! I demand to know what you mean.'

'Now, now, Miss Ballantyne, ask me nicely and I might.'

'No, it would take too long,' she said, in fair imitation of the amorous pretence that he was indulging in.

But it took longer than either anticipated because it wasn't easy to kiss and talk at the same time, and Hanna was too blissfully occupied to question his motives. Only gradually did the truth emerge.

'When I got here this morning the first thing I did was phone Alistair Kerby in London, and I told him to talk some sense into his wife and stop her pestering me. He was only too willing to co-operate.'

'Why did you do that?' she asked.

'Why do you think?' He held her at arm's length and the first flicker of hope crept anxiously into her eyes when they met his.

'You always loved Jessica. You said your world fell apart when she married and you still loved her and didn't want any more complications before you could tell her so.' The words came tumbling out.

'No, Hanna,' he corrected gently, 'you completely misunderstood. I said something happened that shattered my orderly existence. Don't you know that I haven't had a sane moment since I met you? You drive me to distraction!'

'I know, and I'm sorry.'

For some reason the apology made him give a shout of frustration and she made another feeble effort to get away. But he caught one of her hands, turned it upwards and pressed his lips against the palm. 'Don't say you're sorry any more.'

She pulled her hand away and went over to the window. Once Ryan had stood outside there on the balcony in the dark and she had been so aware of him, so pulsatingly conscious of his magnetism she had fled in panic. Her breathing was shallow at the memory. Now he was calling her again, murmuring her name as he had done then, and from habit she felt the need to escape. But he disturbed her deeply and there was sincerity in the way he looked at her.

She turned round slowly. 'The day Jessica got married I tidied up the house after she'd left. I didn't think your photograph ought to be on the bedside table when she got back with Alistair, so I put it in a drawer. There was a letter from you there, begging her to wait before coming to a decision. I didn't mean to read it, but I couldn't help it. Your writing is very clear.'

'And you thought it was a love letter?'

'Yes. I felt so sorry for you. That's why I came over to the studios instead of phoning.'

He came up behind her, circled her waist with his hands and dropped a kiss on top of her head before seeking the sensitive curve of her neck with his mouth.

'I've never written a love letter in my life, and I don't intend us to be apart long enough for me to write one to you,' he said. 'The letter to Jessica was asking her not to stop working on a script I thought particularly good just because we'd had one of our regular differences of opinion. If you'd been indiscreet enough to turn it over and read the beginning you would have seen for yourself. I regretted writing it afterwards because the script never came up to expectations, but it seems it must have been the most important one I've ever sent if it was the means of bringing *you* to me.'

'You don't love her, then?' The tantalising pressure of his lips on her neck set her pulses throbbing.

'I may have done once, before I discovered how unpredictable she is. But never the way I love you. Would I have asked you to marry me otherwise?'

She swung round to face him, her eyes wide with wonder, but there was still a provoking lightness in his tone. 'Stop teasing me, Ryan Donalson!'

For answer he kissed her with a new, vibrant tenderness, easing away every lingering doubt.

'Does that convince you I'm not teasing?'

She hesitated, tilting her head thoughtfully as she gave him an impudent smile. 'Perhaps if we can have just one more re-take I'll be able to let you know.'

'Now who's doing the tormenting? When we're married I'll expect a bit of respect from you.'

'I haven't said yet that I'll marry you.'

'You haven't said yet that you love me, either, but I

know that you do.' He drew her gently into his arms, caressing her. 'Oh, Hanna,' he murmured, all trace of humour gone, 'please say you do, because I love you so much.'

She had no trouble assuring him, whispering the words over and over. But a little later it occurred to her that there was quite a lot he had taken for granted. Not that she wanted to make an issue of it, but one question still seemed to need an answer.

'Ryan, how did you know what decision I'd come to about Jay?'

He gave her one of those self-confident smiles that used to make her cross. 'My darling, if I'd had any doubts at all, right from the beginning, I'd have started a siege of my own!'

She laughed. 'I have a feeling that's what you've been doing already, and you haven't even known me for forty-seven days yet.'

Ryan put his hand to his head in mock despair. 'How will I ever stand it?'

'I don't know. You've warned me once today about not deciding on marriage too quickly.'

'Ah, but we're different,' he said, as though they were the only couple in the world.

The sky was cloudless, a beautiful delphinium blue, and Vicksburg shimmered in the heat of another day, yesterday's storm now nothing but a memory.

'Just think,' said Hanna, 'I won't be standing in the rain with Jay after all. I'll always be with you.'

Then for the first time she took the initiative and reached up to kiss him.

We value your opinion...

You can help us make our books even better by completing and mailing this questionnaire. Please check [✓] the appropriate boxes.

1. Compared to romance series by other publishers, do Harlequin novels have any additional features that make them more attractive?

   .1.1 ☐ yes   .2 ☐ no   .3 ☐ don't know

   If yes, what additional features? _____
   _____
   _____

2. How much do these additional features influence your purchasing of Harlequin novels?

   2.1 ☐ a great deal   .2 ☐ somewhat   .3 ☐ not at all   .4 ☐ not sure

3. Are there any other additional features you would like to include?

   _____
   _____
   _____

4. Where did you obtain this book?

   4.1 ☐ bookstore   .4 ☐ borrowed or traded
   .2 ☐ supermarket   .5 ☐ subscription
   .3 ☐ other store   .6 ☐ other (please specify)_____

5. How long have you been reading Harlequin novels?

   5.1 ☐ less than 3 months   .4 ☐ 1-3 years
   .2 ☐ 3-6 months   .5 ☐ more than 3 years
   .3 ☐ 7-11 months   .6 ☐ don't remember

6. Please indicate your age group.

   6.1 ☐ younger than 18   .3 ☐ 25-34   .5 ☐ 50 or older
   .2 ☐ 18-24   .4 ☐ 35-49

Please mail to: Harlequin Reader Service

In U.S.A.   In Canada
1440 South Priest Drive   649 Ontario Street
Tempe, AZ 85281   Stratford, Ontario N5A 6W2

Thank you very much for your cooperation.

Complete and mail today the FREE gift certificate and subscription reservation on the following pages.

FREE!

A hardcover Romance Treasury volume
containing 3 treasured works of romance
by 3 outstanding Harlequin authors...

..as your introduction to Harlequin's
Romance Treasury subscription plan!

Romance Treasury

...almost 600 pages of exciting romance reading
every month at the low cost of $6.97 a volume!

A wonderful way to collect many of Harlequin's most beautiful love
stories, all originally published in the late '60s and early '70s.
Each value-packed volume, bound in a distinctive gold-embossed
leatherette case and wrapped in a colorfully illustrated dust jacket,
contains...
* 3 full-length novels by 3 world-famous authors of romance fiction
* a unique illustration for every novel
* the elegant touch of a delicate bound-in ribbon bookmark...
  and much, much more!

Romance Treasury

...for a library of romance you'll treasure forever!

Complete and mail today the FREE gift certificate and subscription
reservation on the following page.

Romance Treasury

An exciting opportunity to collect treasured works of romance! Almost 600 pages of exciting romance reading in each beautifully bound hardcover volume!

You may cancel your subscription whenever you wish! You don't have to buy any minimum number of volumes. Whenever you decide to stop your subscription just drop us a line and we'll cancel all further shipments.